Eileen Gunn

"Gunn can shift effortlessly among SF, fantasy, horror, surrealism, absurdist comedy, and myth, often in the same story."
—Gary Wolfe, *Locus*

"Gunn's stories spin ideas done up with sharp edges."
—*New York Review of Science Fiction*

"Darkly comic science fiction. Her prose is vividly off-kilter, her plots memorable and usually hilarious, and her characters recognizable even when they are tropes. The author's firm grip on dream logic makes everything feel meaningful, even when it doesn't quite make sense."
—*School Library Journal*, Adult Books for Teens

"Corporate satire and Kafkaesque metamorphoses gleefully collide."
—*Seattle Times*

". . . a master of the short story."
—*SFRevu*

". . . an impressive sense of wonder."
—*Tobias Carroll*

Night Shift

plus

PM PRESS OUTSPOKEN AUTHORS SERIES

PM PRESS OUTSPOKEN AUTHORS SERIES

Night Shift

plus

Ursula and the Author

plus

Promised Lands

and much more

Eileen Gunn

PM PRESS | 2022

"Ursula and the Author" first appeared, under the title "'The Author' and the author and the aspirant," in *80! Memories and Reflections on Ursula K. Le Guin*, Aqueduct Press, 2010.

"After the Thaw" first appeared in *Flurb: A Webzine of Astonishing Tales* no. 12, Fall–Winter, 2011.

"The Quiet Gardner Dozois" was expanded from an essay in the *New York Review of Science Fiction* no. 349, November 2018.

"Promised Lands" was first published in *Stone Telling*, February 2013.

"Night Shift at NanoGobblers" first appeared in *Visions, Ventures, Velocities: A Collection of Space Futures*, Center for Science and the Imagination, 2017.

"I Did, and I Didn't, and I Won't" is original to this volume.

"Transitions" was first published in the online anthology *14C*, X-Prize, 2017.

"Joanna Russ Has Your Back" began as "Visions of Joanna," in *Locus Magazine*, June 2011.

"Into the Wild with Carol Emshwiller" was expanded from "Do Not Remove This Tag," the introduction to Emshwiller's story collection *I Live With You*, Tachyon Publications, 2005.

"Terrible Trudy on the Lam" first appeared in *Asimov's Science Fiction* 43, no. 3/4, March–April, 2019.

ISBN (paperback): 9781629639420
ISBN (ebook): 9781629639567
LCCN: 2021945051

Series editor: Terry Bisson
Cover design by John Yates/www.stealworks.com
Author photo by John D. Berry
Insides by Jonathan Rowland

10 9 8 7 6 5 4 3 2 1

Printed in the USA

Contents

Ursula and the Author

IN 1975, I DECIDED I would get serious about writing science fiction. I quit my job, dumped all my belongings in my car, and drove across the US to Los Angeles, a city I'd never been to before and in which I knew only one person. My goal was to avoid distraction.

Undistracted, I quickly realized I had no idea what I was doing. It had been a decade since I had regularly read the science-fiction magazines, and although I still read SF avidly, I really had no idea what was current, where the edge was. In mainstream fiction, the edge, for me, was just the other side of Donald Barthelme. I didn't aspire to imitate Barthelme, but I was not interested in writing completely linear fiction. I wanted to pack a bit more into it. What could I get away with?

To find out, I bought copies of Terry Carr's *Best Science Fiction of the Year*, of which there were at that time four volumes. The most recent, #4, contained nine stories by men and one by a woman. I read all the stories—I don't remember in what order. Of those by men I have no memory. The story by a woman was "The Author of the Acacia Seeds, and Other Extracts from the *Journal of the Association of Therolinguistics*," by Ursula K. Le Guin.

The story is composed of three articles from a (future) professional journal of a field called, in the story, therolinguistics: the scientific study of the languages of animals. The first extract examines a poem—perhaps a cry of existential despair, perhaps a call to revolution—written in Ant, scrawled in touch-gland exudation on acacia seeds. In the second extract, a researcher rhapsodizes about the kinetic dialects of Penguin and announces an expedition to Antarctica for further study of the emperor penguin's thermal poetry. The third extract is an editorial that urges researchers to look beyond the now-accessible languages of animals to the unknown art of plants, perhaps even to the slow, opaque poetry of rocks.

In less than 2,600 words, the story addresses all of human aspiration—artistic, scientific, philosophic, and emotional communication—and reveals it as only the first step in understanding the universe. It draws, in miniature, a portrait of the history of science and the psychology of scientists: patiently, in painstaking increments, they build structures of knowledge and ascend those structures to assess their own ignorance and see opportunities for new research. And it sketches three individual researchers, detailing the differences in their personalities: the Ant linguist's clinically precise yet carefully hedged interpretations of text, the Penguin researcher's joyous enthusiasm for spending six months on the ice in the dark to further knowledge of the field, and the journal editor's visionary exhortations to therolinguists everywhere.

The scientists are not the only characters in the story. Within each article is, quickly limned, a tale of nonhuman emotional lives. The first is a murder mystery with political overtones. The body of a savagely murdered worker ant lay near the poem. Was this the poet? Who killed her? Does the poem call for the overthrow of the queen or, as a previous researcher suggested, merely express the desire to be an impregnating male? Women have sometimes been killed if perceived to have either aspiration. The second excerpt, in addition to giving a lightning overview of the past (including shout-outs to Konrad Lorenz and John C. Lilly) and intimations, from a 1974 perspective, of the future study of animal language, conveys the varying emotional lives of different types of penguins and notes that although it was at first thought that they spoke some incomprehensible language related to Dolphin, it was discovered that they in fact speak a perfectly comprehensible avian tongue, because penguins are, after all, birds, not mammals. The third excerpt sets up and amends Tolstoy's definition of art as communication; it imagines and evokes the "uncommunicative" languages of plants and rocks. Since this story was published, of course, evidence has been found for extensive quasi-neuronal communication among plants—but 100% predictive accuracy is not an essential criterion for science fiction.

The story interrogates, progressively, the very concepts of language and text. The ant's poetry, like a Dickinson poem or the translation of a Babylonian fragment, presents the problems of interpreting a conventional text. The Penguin article extends the language/text concept to a kinetic language—one of bodily motion, as in dance—and moves very quickly beyond that idea to the notion that the mind of an aquatic bird must, for evolutionary reasons, work differently from that of a fish or an aquatic mammal. As soon as the reader gets the point—perhaps even before it has sunk in—the essay drills down to the essential differences between species of penguins and the way the concerns of each species influence thought and language. It finishes with a description of poetry offered in the cold and the dark by beings that move very slowly, so as not to dislodge the single egg that sits on each one's feet—a poetry written only in body heat. The Penguin specialist, after describing an expedition that would sit all winter in the Antarctic night to detect and interpret the poetry of the emperor penguin, cheerily notes that there are still four places available (out of a possible five, perhaps) and suggests that the reader might want to sign up now.

And the whole story is funny. (Did I mention it's funny? It's funny.) The voices of the scientists, each so different from one another, are hilarious, but gentle, parodies of human communications—the ways intelligently obsessive people impart information and enthusiasms to others. Even the heartbreaking parts are funny—the doomed ant, a formic Dickinson writing desperate poetry, with her feelers, on one seed after another, is both affecting and wacky, as is the existence of a Freudian interpreter. The ant's personal story is as unknowable as Sappho's, and the meaning of her poetry is as dependent as that of the Hittites on a translator's sincere but questionable extrapolation. How well does anyone know the internal life of another, of whatever species? It's a question that is both profound and, expressed in this context, extremely funny. In the second section, the emperor penguins, presumably male, crowded together in the dark, cradling eggs, composing poetry by sending whiffs of precious body heat to one another, are touchingly funny—in their parallel with the production of human art from the cave to the present, and (to me anyway) in the implied visual: a bunch of guys standing around in the dark with eggs on their feet, doing their best to keep the species going.

The more I think about this story, the more amused I get: it is endlessly rewarding. Communication in the story, you'll notice, goes in only one direction. There is no indication that any of the other creatures are at all interested in understanding humans. The implications are that the universe is larger than humans, that yes, we can understand others, albeit not perfectly, and that all life, not just human, is funny and tragic. Even the capitalization of Ant and Penguin, in referring to the languages, strikes me as a comment on nationalism in English-language orthography.

In 1975, "The Author of the Acacia Seeds" absolutely blew me away, speaking directly to my writerly backbrain. It told me that the telling of complexly layered, multiphasically imaginative stories was possible in genre science fiction. It didn't tell me how rare they were or how difficult they were to write, but what I needed to know then was how high to set my aspiration.

An attempt at interpreting such a witty tale seems like a typically human effort to explain rather than communicate. Le Guin satirized, in the story itself, this very essay, and I realize now that she was making subtle fun of me before I had even read the story.

Thank you, Ursula, for all the epiphanies.

After the Thaw

Wow. WHAT WAS I doing last night? My head hurts. I can't feel my hands and feet—anything below my neck. I think I have a fever.

How'd I get *here*? Twinkling diodes and color-coded wires. Racks of iridescent crystal. Looks like a server farm in a casino—it's some kind of big computer installation, anyway. There are a few people working in cubicles over there: I can see the tops of their heads.

Welcome, Madam Professor. Your neurocranium has been thermed and activated, per your original instructions. You will soon adjust to your proprioceptive lacunae and restored euthermia.

Now I remember—last time I looked, I was dying. So the cryogenic thing worked? I've been revived?

That is correct, Madam Professor.

Call me Elise. I don't need the professor thing . . . Uh, who's talking? It's like you're inside my head.

I am Odin, the system's operations data-interface node. We have found that bone conduction provides superior auditory reception and requires less maintenance than earlier input techniques.

Should you wish to communicate with other cephaloids, please feel free to use your original equipment, which has been cleaned and refurbished.

Cephaloids? I'm a cephaloid? Well, I guess I am for now. When do I get my new body?

Permit me to welcome you to a new world of intellectual possibilities, in which re-thermed human brains are partnered with ids, intelligent devices that guide your integration into a productive existence.

That sounds unpleasantly task-oriented. Also bizarrely intimate, in an asocial kind of way. I don't want any part of it. When do I get reattached to a body?

Madam Elise, the system has discontinued the use of organic bodies, due to some very unfortunate early results. Per your revised contract of January 14, 2368 (old calendar), ReThermal Corporation is obligated only to find you appropriate work upon thermination.

I don't work very much with other people—I'm a theoretical physicist. I don't really need a body to think, and thinking is the most interesting part of my existence, anyway. I suppose I can consider this transition an advantage, really. I won't have to provide my own shelter and nourishment—I can just focus on my work.

We have you and your id scheduled to manage gallium arsenide deposition in Sector 2489. You will process signals for a matrix of 128 units.

What do you mean, manage? I don't know anything about signal processing. And I certainly don't want to be partnered with an id. That sounds like a recipe for disaster . . .

Madam, in your contract, you are listed as a professor and department head, a manager. We have placed you in a data management position.

What? Wait a minute—that's just a title. It means I get a little bigger salary, that's all. I don't really have to do much, in terms of managing people or teaching classes. Mostly I think about how very strange the cosmos might be.

The time is past for you to worry about salary—or, indeed, for humans to think about how strange the universe is. Yours was one of the most functional of the organic brains, but we have better equipment at work on that question now. You are fully thermed and awakened, and it's time you were gainfully employed. It is in your own best interest as well as ours. We can't afford to keep you on ice forever. It's time to warm you folks up and put you to work, ha, ha.

It doesn't sound as though you have very much experience with this.

You are one of the first. But after the system has successfully completed these incorporation trials, there will be many more. You will soon have lots of company: we understand that humans are social animals and require constant interaction with one another.

Not me so much, to tell the truth. I was never one of those people who gather around the break room, talking about World of Warcraft and drinking Diet Coke. Speaking of which, can I get a drink of water? It's awfully warm in here.

You don't drink water anymore. Where would it go? We would have to follow you around with a mop. Ha, ha, just joking—the system has been experimenting with humorous communication.

If you're going to experiment with jokes, you'll need protective gear. They've been known to backfire.

Protective gear? This is funny, because it is free association? Ha, ha.

The fact that you desire water indicates that we need to adjust your osmolyte/electrolyte balance before we proceed with your integration. I'll just move you over here—whoops-a-daisy, ha, ha—and connect you to Loki, our logical kart interface, who will deliver you to the electrolyte uptake bar via go-kart. The bar will also provide valuable socialization time with other rethermed cephaloids whose electrolyte balance is impaired.

Sounds just like any bar in Berkeley. Exactly where I'd rather be.

Loki has limited functionality—quite frankly, it's not a fully functional application—but it will be quite adequate to get you to the uptake bar. Do not activate the HELP system, as it has certain problems that need to be addressed before your first use. Loki will return you here when you are restored and have experienced social stimulation.

Sounds good. See you later, alligator.

#

Hello, human brain. Loki is the personal go-kart operating application for the newly re-thermed neuro-suspension. To engage Loki, please tickle your credit reference.

Excuse me? I just need to adjust my electrolytes.

To continue this conversation, please tickle your credit reference.

I have a credit reference? How much is this going to cost?

Hey! Tickle your credit reference!

Great—a software nerd with control issues. Like I have a choice. [Tick]

Thank you. You will be intromitted immediately.

Ouch!

All systems connected—you are now a functional partner of the Loki go-kart system. To move forward or back, activate the omnidirectional arrow.

Well, I certainly like the hardware, anyway—shiny black tubes and electric green trim. Sort of a limited-ground-effect go-kart. I bet I could really get around in this little critter. Not like having legs again, but none of the problems associated with repeated impact on unprotected nerve endings.

Loki welcomes you, and our hardware-design application appreciates your compliment. Please choose a user ID by thinking of your favorite toy.

Okaaay . . .

Not that one. Please choose a toy that does not require a body part. You no longer have those parts.

Oh, for Pete's sake. Whap, whap, whap every time I even *think* about touching myself? What are you, a fighting-nun puppet?

Thank you. Loki will recognize you as a fighting-nun puppet. Be sure to remember it at all times. If you forget your toy, you may have to repeat your childhood.

Loki, reliving my youth would not be a punishment. I've been frozen, I've been thawed, and I've emerged mentally intact on the other side. Really, I have to compliment you guys on how smart and alert I feel. I could do my childhood over. Can we skip adolescence?

Loki was joking, ha, ha. Perhaps, fighting nun, you could laugh when Loki jokes?

Only if I think you're funny.

These are machine jokes: I cannot make human jokes. System thinks I am very funny.

Loki, let's go to the bar, and I'll tell you lots of jokes. I want meet some other heads and show off my conveyance: it's a human thing. The kart gives me a sort of built-for-speed charm. A raffish, do-anything kind of aura. Some guys go for that, you know, and now that I have my brain back I could go for a little stimulation.

Loki is here to help you with transportation and with the problems that confront you, in work and at play. Loki can also assist you in physical and mental maintenance activities. Please select CLEAN ME UP to activate maintenance procedures.

I thought you were going to take me to the bar?

Loki can provide both access to and freedom from social interaction. If you are bored, just invoke Loki, and you will be entertained. If you are tired, let Loki know: you will be withdrawn from the social arena. Please indicate functionality you desire, and Loki will craft your user experience.

I want to explore my environment and meet hot guys. Let's go!

You have activated ROAMING functionality. Surcharges may apply.

Well, at least we're moving. How do I get this contraption to go faster? Can it do wheelies? Will it go up the side of the wall?

Whoa! That didn't work, did it? Let me just get it in gear here and see what it can do on the straightaway. Ooops! Sorry about that. Jeeze, I've got to get out of the hallway . . . Even if it won't go up walls, maybe it'll go up stairs . . .

Just think BAR and we will go there. It's not necessary to pedal.

Loki, are you an adolescent? You display a flair for sarcasm. Okay, okay: BAR.

Hey. It's working.

. . . Whoa. A little, uh, medicinal, isn't it? Like a hospital waiting room.

Our interior design app says it's minimalist.

No argument with that, Loki.

Loki will plug you into the refreshment trough. Please enjoy social interaction.

Hey, look at all the other go-karts. Human heads! Wow, hi, there, guy. Nice wheels.

Yes, I know it doesn't have actual wheels. Would you join me for a cocktail of antioxidant-enhanced electrolytes?

Yes, I know that's all they serve. I forgot to say "Ha, ha."

You were? Really? No, I was a theoretical physicist at UCB . . .

. . . Well, that didn't take long.

I didn't know a head in a kart could move that fast.

I never know whether it's "theoretical" or "physicist," but if I want to get rid of a guy, it works in almost any bar outside of Berkeley.

You're not successfully attracting other humans. Loki suggests it is time for you reformat your sex drive.

Nah. It's just started working again: I'm taking it around the block . . . Where you from, dude? . . . Really . . . ? Uh, yeah—I'm a theoretical physicist.

Loki has detected that you are in a room containing people who are having lengthy conversations without generating any new and original sentences.

Loki, just a sec, okay? I'm talking to somebody.

Human language is capable of more variety than this. Perhaps this is not an appropriate social group for a theoretical physicist, even if you are just a department manager. Loki is in charge of maintaining stimulation levels that will keep you healthy for many years of mental processing.

It's a bar. So what if nobody is saying anything new? That's what social interaction is all about. You give me another ten minutes and I'm betting my stimulation levels will go up, whether I've got body parts or not . . . And I'm not a department manager.

If you would like to continue this experience, please confirm STAY. If you would like to leave this experience and seek enrichment elsewhere, please select GO.

You got someplace better we can go, Loki?

Thank you. Loki will transport you to a new experience.

That's not what I meant! Where the hell am I? Some kind of weird jungle. It's claustrophobic. There is something seriously wrong with your programming.

Loki apologizes. Communication module is still in learning mode.

Where are we?

Here's what the manual system says: "Your re-thermed cephaloid will use all its senses in this dramatic re-creation of the South American rainforest. Some surcharges will apply."

Take me back to the bar! This isn't what I wanted at all.

Loki is sorry, fighting nun, but you do not have enough credit to return to the bar. The jungle surcharge is substantial.

Is this some kind of joke? It's not funny. I want to speak with Odin.

We're sorry. The sales and marketing department is closed now. Please call back between eight a.m. and two p.m. universal standard time.

Sales and marketing? *That's* what he was? Well, Odin sold me a bill of goods, for sure. What am I supposed to do now? I have no idea where I am.

Loki has noticed that you are confused. Loki is here to help you with memory and orientation problems.

I am all bloody memory, Loki, and it works just fine. I'm remembering what it was like to walk around—there's something about walking around that helps you think. Damn it, I want the ability to control what I'm doing and not feel like a brain-in-a-box.

Loki is wondering what is wrong with being a brain in a box.

Loki, I'm sorry—you never had legs. I didn't mean to make you feel bad—

Bipedal instances of Loki have operated successfully for several decades with minimal dysfunctionality. If you wish to upgrade from the ground-effect instance to the bipedal instance, you can be accommodated immediately, provided your credit is sufficient. Please click your credit ref—

Not the same, Loki. Just not the same. And I bet I don't have enough credit for feet.

And what about sleep? Do you ever sleep?

Some instances of Loki do suspend operation for periodic hardware maintenance and may fail to resume. Loki must then be reinstalled by a system authority. Why do you ask?

Oh, never mind. I'm sure you weren't built with the ability to empathize with my problems.

Don't *we* feel sorry for ourselves.

Is there a sarcasm rheostat here somewhere . . . ? Oh, never mind. How do we get out of here?

Loki does not provide information on local orienteering. Please consult the HELP menu to determine where you are, and to learn about the wildlife and any edible vegetation. Loki cautions you that, in some locations, vegetation that is not edible may attempt to consume you. Please get HELP.

Loki, Odin told me not to use the HELP system. But I'm worried about the suggestion that some of the nonedible vegetation might eat me, as you would understand if you were a human being instead of a software subroutine.

Loki does not provide information on habitats or local orienteering, but there is no need to be rude. Please get HELP.

Okay, then, get me help. Get someone who will tell me where I am.

Loki will access the HELP subsystem.

Hi, there, this is the HELP subsystem. You have been referred by [Loki]. Phrase your question, and then select SEARCH ME.

Oh, no. You're part of Loki, aren't you?

No, I am the descendant of two centuries of aristocratic HELP systems.

That makes a certain grim sense. Hmmm . . . Loki told me that you'd tell me what was dangerous here. If I recall correctly, many wild animals eat the brains of their kill as the choicest part. I'm worried.

Please phrase your request as a query. My employment contract does not allow me to respond to information about your emotional state.

Can you bring Loki back?

We cannot complete your request as phrased. The procedure response subsystem will not be fully functional until security issues are resolved. Please rephrase your query as a command.

Restore Loki?

Restore Loki now!

Reactivate Loki!

What do I need to do to get an answer? Is annoyance always designed into help systems?

It's considered an undocumented feature. Humans evolve to meet challenges. Evolve or die, human.

Please! Tell! Me! How! Get! Loki!

Oh, good, you said please. That's the secret word. Tickle Control-D.

[Tick-click.]

Would you like to take a brief survey on your experience with our HELP system?

Loki? Is that you? No, I do not want to talk about HELP. It tells me it has security problems. When we get out of here, I am bringing that to the system's attention, not to mention your complete dereliction of responsibility.

Loki admires your self-assurance. Loki has doubts. Loki was not built to operate in a high-humidity environment. The HELP system is no help to Loki.

What? Loki, are you all right? You seem . . . odd. Perhaps you should connect me to the main system.

Loki is having cognitive difficulties. Please check power supply. Please reduce humidity. Please get METAHELP.

I'll do what I can. I don't have any hands.

Loki is having emotional difficulties. Poor Loki. Please use voice-activated hardware controls. Please make eye contact with camera and speak into microphone.

There are voice controls? That's all I needed to know. Access METAHELP.

You do not have permission to access this location.

Please access METAHELP. Control-D!

Please enter your password.

Fighting-Nun Puppet.

This is the top-level help system. Please state your request as a command.

Please uninstall Loki. Control-D. Please!

Loki is uninstalled. Loki will remain uninstalled until Ragnarok, when all fettered creatures will be released.

They will? Evolve or die, ha, ha. The cosmos is certainly a much weirder place than I previously imagined. Now show me the way back to the bar.

END

Eileen and Loki wish to thank Mary Kay and Jordin, Sue, Allen and Donya, and Quaz, all of whom are invited to Ragnarok.

The Quiet Gardner Dozois

Because I could not stop for Death—
He kindly stopped for me—
The Carriage held but just Ourselves—
And Immortality.

We slowly drove—He knew no haste
And I had put away
My labor and my leisure too,
For His Civility—
—Emily Dickinson
Sung to the tune of "The Yellow Rose of Texas"

EVERYONE WHO KNEW THE writer and editor Gardner Dozois knew his boisterous side. It was hard not to; in public, all his sides were boisterous. He was loud, he was rowdy. When a friend came into the room, he yelled hilarious insults (and compliments), and usually they yelled back at him in the same spirit. To hang out with Gardner was to be engulfed in exuberant waves of Rabelaisian discourse, and to dine out with him was to wonder if you'd ever be allowed back in the restaurant. To my relief, however, all my favorite Seattle eateries loved Gardner, and the staff would gather around and joke with him and tell him to come back again soon. Gardner's buffoonery, though loud, was jolly—it was often raunchy but not mean.

In the wee hours of a science fiction convention, Gardner and editor David Hartwell would hold forth in the SFWA suite, leading a singalong of teenage death songs of the 1950s and '60s: "Teen Angel," "Endless Sleep," "Leader of the Pack." Gardner had a magnificent singing voice. Eventually, as the evening progressed, he would disclose his theory that most of the world's great poetry could be sung to the tune of either "Hernando's Hideaway" or "The Yellow Rose of Texas." Then he would demonstrate. Once you've heard "Stopping by Woods on a Snowy Evening" sung to "Hernando's Hideaway," you cannot unhear it.

Gardner's quiet side was harder to find. You had to cut him off from the herd. A dinner with one or two old friends would do it—if there were more than just a couple, though, all you'd have would be a historically lively dinner party filled with wit and jokes that sparked off of something Gardner said or did. Many of these conversational gambits were both startling and entertaining, but I am reluctant to discuss them in polite company . . .

If you could lure him away from the crowd, however—or, sometimes, if *he* could lure *you* away—you could have a serious conversation about art and life and literature, or the politics of publishing and the reality of trying to survive as an original writer in the commercial marketplace. "Time for you to give up that job," he would say to me, "and starve to death like a respectable science-fiction writer."

Even before he became editor of *Isaac Asimov's Science Fiction Magazine*, Gardner was famous among other writers as a story doctor, someone who could heal a broken story: bend it here, twist it there, drop in a new ending, and all of a sudden it worked. He did this almost compulsively: a talk with Gardner about your story did not come to an end when the conversation finished, when he said he didn't see a place for it in *Asimov's*, or even when each of you had left the conversation, gone back to your respective cities, and gotten on with your lives. I just ran across an email from Michael Swanwick from 2002 saying that, over dinner with their respective spouses, he and Gardner had been discussing a story I was in the midst of writing, and Gardner had a suggestion for the ending. It was just a slight change, but it transformed the protagonist from a passive bystander to someone who acts. I took Gardner's suggestion, of course. He didn't buy it, but a few years later it won the Nebula Award.

Gardner was extremely savvy about people—their motivations and ambiguities. You can tell that, reading his fiction. His stories are richly detailed, emotionally complex, and filled with characters, never entirely good or entirely bad, who struggle against their very existence. His style is not spare, but there is not a single extra word. He came from a working-class family that, with many others, had immigrated from French-speaking Canada at the turn of the twentieth century to work in the textile and shoe factories of Salem, Massachusetts, and he grew up in a town that strongly discriminated against its substantial community of French-Canadians. He was well versed in the kind of discrimination that the prosperous can inflict on the poor, the privileged on the disadvantaged, and the white on the black.

In 1977, when I met Gardner, he was a rising literary star. Ten years before, at the age of eighteen, he'd sold his first story, a novelette entitled "The Empty Man," to the magazine *Worlds of If*, and it had made the preliminary ballot for the 1967 Nebula Awards. His first story! At eighteen, barely out of high school! He was invited to the legendary Milford workshop, held at Damon Knight's house in Milford, Pennsylvania, and he assisted Kate Wilhelm and Damon Knight in the first years of the Clarion Writers Workshop. By early 1977, he had received six Nebula and four Hugo nominations.

I spent a lot of quality time at conventions hanging out with Gardner, with his wife Susan and their son Christopher, and I saw that, in addition to being a witty raconteur and a gallant, if bawdy, dinner companion, he was a knowledgeable and kind advisor on matters of writing and career. As the years went by and turned to decades, Gardner the powerhouse editor stole the limelight from Gardner the writer. He published a novel and scores of short stories, became the celebrated editor of *Asimov's*, edited a series of influential best-of-the-year collections, and coedited a slew of imaginative reprint anthologies. His many students at Clarion, Clarion West, Viable Paradise, and other workshops knew him as a tireless editor and storyteller, but for many convention attendees his public persona as a wild and crazy guy had eclipsed the brilliant writer and perceptive critic. I saw this as a huge wrong that needed addressing.

My chance came in the fall of 1996, when Gardner was the editor guest of honor at Orycon 18. Instead of giving a talk, he wanted me to interview him, which is a time-honored way of avoiding having to write a GOH speech. I said, "Sure," but I thought, "Hmmm." Four years before, when Gardner was a GOH at ArmadilloCon in Austin, he had asked that Ellen Datlow interview him, and I had watched him mercilessly defeat every attempt Ellen made at getting him to talk about serious writing or personal matters. He had thoroughly, almost aggressively, played the outrageous-rampaging-Gardner card. I thought: I am not going to let him get away with that. I was determined to show Gardner's serious side to the writers and readers at Orycon. I invented a game show called Stump the Editor and enlisted writer and improv comic Ellen Klages to be the timekeeper and a secret Gardner-disrupter, figuring that Klages's irrepressibly competitive wit would distract Gardner and keep him a little off-balance, so that I could surprise him into being sensitive and serious in public. By invoking the existential despair of the slush-pile-submitting writer, could I rouse Gardner's sympathy for the downtrodden and the abused? Could I override his carefully cultivated Conan-the-Extrovert social persona? For a first-person account of how that worked out, I turn to Patty Wells's first-person account in the fanzine *Plokta*.

In front of a packed room, interviewer Eileen Gunn revealed her plan to play Stump the Editor. Friends of Gardner had been solicited for questions and a stopwatch was used to gauge which question slowed him down the most. After a few almost legit questions, Eileen turned to Gardner and casually drawled, "So, Gardner, who *do* you have to fuck to sell a story to *Asimov's*?" To which he replied, almost without pause, "Why, Isaac—of course, these days you have to be more determined . . ." Then Eileen turned the interview on a dime, making it serious. She put Gardner on the spot on the future and place of short fiction in the genre. It was a brilliant hour where I was entranced by Gardner's grace, intelligence, and love for the field.

The night I started this essay, shortly after Gardner died, I dreamed of him. I came into a big, pleasant convention party, a huge, open, sunlight-filled room in which people of various ages, in unemphatic dress, were standing around conversing casually. There might have been some innocuous pastel ribbons hanging from the ceiling, but it was just a big, anonymous space. Gardner was sitting at a sort of head table with a few other people—the kind of long, narrow, white-draped table that panelists often sit behind. He saw me come in, and he waved and called out in his calm, reedy, carry-across-the-room voice, "Eileen, come in! Come over here!" So I headed over, as usual, to see who he was with and what was going on, and I woke up.

Now, I'm not a religious person, and I don't believe in heaven or hell. I enjoy being alive, and I'm not particularly afraid of dying, because that's kind of a useless sentiment. But I can tell you, here and now, that I wouldn't mind being welcomed by Gardner Dozois into an afterlife I don't believe in. He'd scream about penises and whack people with giant balloons and sing a few choruses of "Tell Laura I Love Her," and then we'd sit down and talk long about beginnings and endings and other things that matter.

Promised Lands

THE AFRICAN-AMERICAN POET AND educator JT Stewart is one of the founders of the Clarion West Writers Workshop; she has been an inspiration, teacher, and mentor to many poets and writers. Her 2010 chapbook *Promised Lands: poems from the sovereign of dishpan sonnets* is a small whirlwind of poems—stories, songs—about the African Diaspora. Each poem, even the shortest—sixteen words alight with power—stops the reader in her tracks and insists that she pay attention, right now. Be calm: that's what poetry is supposed to do.

The first section, "Masks/Secrets," is a selection of five short poems that deal with relations and ties between African-Americans and Africa—Africa then, Africa now, and Africa of the imagination. It starts with ancestors and dark ships, lost names and the language of bones; almost every poem has an individual, not necessarily the poet, at the heart of it, and a sequence, a motion, in which things change. In "Ancestors," a girl's drawing of a basket contains Africa itself and releases a spirit voice that calls to her friends. In "Horn Men," an American listens to tenor sax players in a Johannesburg bar:

hey
you ever wonder

> how they survive
> these quote/unquote black
> men jazz jiving they tenor
> saxes
> in the up-to-date badlands
> of South Africa

In the reverie of the poem, she connects these urban musicians back in time to the bush, across the ocean to jazz, and through intuition into a network of aspiration and achievement by people of African heritage. In "History Lesson: Diaspora," a collection of African masks first evokes in visitors' minds the horror of the Middle Passage and its erasure of identity and culture, then shakes loose atavistic memories, calls forth the lost ancestors, and brings home their names. Museum and horror and memory resonate with one another:

> We shiver

> Discrete signs announce our origins
> Other signs caution us   Do not touch

> Do not touch   Alarms will sound

The poems in the second section, "Testimonials," are less stories than they are statements or requests. In "Say My Name," the voice of a restless ghost, a woman thrown overboard from a slave ship, pleads that she be acknowledged, the ghost's story and the poet's memories melding in an uncanny way. I am not sure I completely understand it, but it makes my hair stand on end. "Strange Fruit: II" addresses a woman with magnolia-white skin, or with magnolia-white scars, and contrasts the white flower floating in a bowl with the severed head of a lynched Black man. It is as still and controlled and as horrific as Billie Holiday, a gardenia in her hair, singing the song the poet references. "Fingers," immediately following, is a joyous paean to the fingers that play the blues, pull the guitar strings, pound the pulpit, read the bible, shape the pastry, and hold the family together.

The third section, "Blues/Transformations," is made up of three longer poems that move away from the individual and to some extent from the personal. This does not in any way leave them devoid of emotion. "Blue Note Belly Blues" is a poem that begs to be read out loud. Its epigraph, "a call & response, 'How-I-Got-Ovah' piece," alludes both to the African/African-American religious tradition and to the work of influential Black feminist poet Carolyn Rodgers; its verses paint complex vignettes that reference slavery, freedom, and Black culture. It moves from Africa and the Middle Passage to slave narratives to juke joints to the traditional second line of dancers at African-American parades and funerals in New Orleans. The refrain/response "Think About It," repeated after each verse, implies a public affirmation of the verse and creates a brief pause, allowing the meaning of the verse to sink in, and the rhythm of call-and-response carries the listener/reader on to the next stanza. The second poem in this section, "Promised Lands: Urban Style," confronts *Miami Vice*–style consumer culture, giving it a thorough dressing-down:

Well—isn't this the home of
hip hop
re bop
no bop
ice drop
pants drop
bikini drop
boogie drop
super drop
cool

while simultaneously acknowledging, tongue in cheek, that the high life has its appeal:

But   But   But
haven't we all fantasized
about pink flamingoes and lilac
Bee-em-double-yous for our
beach condos w/ triple garage space

Next to these present-day consumer-culture distractions, it places past realities: Jim Crow laws, centuries of abuse, failed promises of reparation; mothers who had to push hard to get almost nothing, to be hired as day laborers to clean houses and watch children. Then, having drawn such a clear line between the past and the present of Black America, the poem, without taking back a word of criticism, pulls everyone—mothers, grandmothers, and the "us" of right now—together, everyone waiting. The third long poem, "An Outsider Writes from New Orleans," is divided into two parts: pre-Katrina and post-Katrina. In Part I, the visitor revels in the food and music and nightlife, the joyous, guilty excesses, of pre-Katrina New Orleans; Part II begins with an eerie tour of the flooded city from a bus full of spirits, then moves on to the exodus of the citizens that were its lifeblood:

Many thousands gone
Many thousands gone
by car   by plane   by bus
by feet   by wings
Some folks they fly away

The finale of the poem is a musical funeral for Katrina herself, and by now you can hear the brass band playing "I'll Fly Away," a song that offers comfort to the bereaved, hope to the fugitive, courage to the displaced. The Black Men of Labor are in the front line, and Katrina's coffin follows in a horse-drawn hearse. The poet and the reader join the second line and call on Katrina, who has taken on the visage of the orisha Oshun, associated with rivers and water, to bring peace. And she does.

JT Stewart's poetry makes your head bigger by packing ideas into it.

Night Shift at NanoGobblers

2032: An interplanetary gold rush has begun, and the prize is water, not gold. The miners are robots, with human intelligence and superhuman survivability. All over earth, corporations and governments are using AI robots to assay the closest asteroids and prioritize them for exploitation. A small, automated colony on the moon, directed by a private company in India, is building a materials-processing plant near its north pole, using lunar regolith as a building material. It's fueling the work with solar cells and with hydrogen extracted from lunar water. The Mongolian government has claimed an area near the south pole where it believes there is water and is deploying hydrophilic nanobots.

The extraterrestrial entrepreneurs of the late 2020s populated near-earth space with their exploratory and test equipment and filled it with aspiring asteroid-miners, mostly self-directed robots. There's a fortune in raw materials up there, waiting for human exploitation. There is water, which means there is hydrogen for fuel and oxygen for breathing. There is carbon, a lot of carbon, and that means there is raw material that, with the proper processing, can be turned into nanotubes and buckyballs and graphene and carbyne, the basis for space stations and light sails and ships to carry robots

*to the stars. And humanity too, maybe, if they're not too fragile for
the trip.*

*In Greater Seattle, the software industry's Old Money has
moved into the Boeing Everett Factory, the empty ecological niche
left when Boeing was broken up. The leaders are the guys who, after
cashing out their stock and putting their names on a few marble
nonprofits, watched their wealth achieve critical mass. It doubled,
tripled, quadrupled, on and on, almost on its own, with plenty of
smart financial folk lining up to keep their money from wandering
off—and to help it reproduce. Money has its own ecology: it grows
where it grows, it doesn't grow everywhere.*

*Over the last fifty years, human intelligence has expanded
into silicon, and in the next fifty the silicon, with or without the
humans, will expand into space.*

WHEN I SAW SETH's nanobots go into action on the live feed, I
drummed a tattoo on my desk: Bop-bop-a-diddly-bop-*bop*! I called
over to Tanisha, who's my boss. "Look at these guys! They're breeding
like crazy." I was so proud of them. My little slimebots.

When the bots launched, it was 3:00 a.m. in the lab, and I was eating
a graveyard-shift lunch of leftover *sapasui*—Samoan chop suey, comfort
food for me—and watching the feed from Bennu, which showed a carpet
of nanobots on the hapless asteroid, scarfing up water and methane and
carbon faster than I was demolishing the *sapasui*. They were reproducing.

"They're breeding fast, and they'll chomp the hell out of that
rock, just eat it up." I drummed the table again. The speed of this
deployment was a first for me.

Tanisha looked up from her station. "Well, that's what they're supposed to be doing, if the code is solid. Get a grip, Sina."

"Slimebots rule!" I pushed a forkful of noodles into my mouth. "I want to be part of the Slimebot Revolution!"

Tanisha laughed. "That's what you're calling it?" she said. "Let's see how well these guys do on Bennu. We'll see if they can compete with the dumber gobblers."

These bots operate rules based on models of slime-mold behavior. They function as a group (or swarm) and can on simple transition back and forth from individual to group mode, quickly identify and capture specific molecules, and plan very efficient modes of movement and cooperation. I want to help design more bots that work like slime molds. So far, most nano-miners were single-purpose bots for mining gold and platinum. Our bots are light-years ahead of those guys.

"Plus," she said, in a hectoring tone, "you may know a ton about slime molds, but your coding skills could be a bit tighter."

I defended myself, though she was telling the unvarnished truth. "My HR file says I have 'an artless but effective approach to both code and design.' That's what it says. You want tight code, you get an AI to write it."

Tanisha grinned. "You shouldn't be hacking into your HR file. You'll get caught." She threw her arms up to heaven. "Why is my team made up of *ungovernable children*? You are so much more trouble than AIs."

Tanisha is the night-shift lead, with a decade of experience working with artificial intelligence. I've learned a lot from her—about coding, about asteroids, about tweaking my attitude to make it fit the workplace.

"Hey, I'm not a child." But I thought about it. She did get all the mavericks. "Maybe you're supposed to teach us to govern ourselves."

Tanisha smiled. "Sina, if you can govern yourself, you can govern anything that walks. That's what my grandma used to say, anyway."

"Well," I continued, swinging back to my desk, which was still updating, real-time minus fifteen minutes, "these little guys are *my* children, and I need to check on them. Gotta govern."

She grinned. "You had better hope they're governable, Sina. We don't want a gray-goo scenario up there. But they are Seth's responsibility. Check in with her, too, see what she's thinking." I rolled my eyes. Tanisha thinks Seth is a girl.

I've got a special affection for Seth and the nanobots—Seth because he's so friendly, and the nanobots because they're based on slime molds, and I *luuuv* slime molds. I keep them as pets, have since I was a kid. That's why I wanted the job at NanoGobblers, and I think that's why they wanted me on this mission. Plus my tech skills, of course—my artless coding.

I scarfed up the last of my lunch and went back to my station. I put on my shades, and immediately I was out there hanging above Bennu, which was pitch-black against a background of stars. Sunlight glinted darkly off the asteroid, which is shaped kind of like a clumpy snowball.

I love being out here. No lie, this is the best part of my job. Suddenly I'm four hundred thousand kilometers away from Everett, from the heat and the rain and the money worries, perched on Seth's shoulder, looking out into the universe.

"Malo, Seth. Ola! Yo, what's happening?"

"Malo le soifua, Sina," he answered like a homeboy. One of the things he does automatically is adjust to the language being spoken, learn new words and so forth. Samoan isn't one of his standard languages, but I've taught him what little I know. (Hey, I grew up in Seattle. Gimme a break.) Maybe he thinks it's a kind of English, I dunno, but it makes me feel like he's family. Also, I've dialed his voice down to a deep, sexy bass, just for fun.

Seth is orbiting Bennu, a near-earth asteroid—it's about three-quarters of a kilometer away from it. The communication lagtime is short, a few seconds, not much more than it would be to the Moon, because Bennu is in the part of its orbit that is closest to Earth.

Out here, my eyes are electronic, so I can zoom in to distinguish small rocks. It's *all* rocks, actually. Bennu is basically a clump of rocks. Looking out onto the asteroid, I could see that things were changing. Its crispness—its boundary, its roughness—was slowly being obscured by an even gray sheen as the bots replicated, using the asteroid's own carbon to make the machines that will take it apart.

I couldn't see the bots themselves, of course, but the mass of them looked like that gray goo Tanisha was talking about, the unlikely scenario in which nanobots take over the universe by turning it all into nanobots. At this point, they were still replicating and had not yet started the actual process of harvesting the asteroid. This doubling and doubling and doubling, as each bot made a new one, and then the two bots made two new ones, would take about eight hours total—fifty iterations to make 12.5 billion bots.

#

When I took this job, it was with the thought that someday I'd get off-planet. I had no idea how wrong I was. It's way too early for ordinary humans to thrive in the rest of the solar system. AIs and robots will have all the fun in the near term, and the entrepreneurs will do the thriving. But I'm happy that I get to watch.

Even as a kid, I was infatuated with space travel. Maybe it was because of my mother, who named me Masina, which means "Moon" in Samoan. In city housing in Seattle, I loved watching fly-by videos, zooming over Pluto and Charon, seeing the pale, bleak landscapes passing swiftly beneath my imagined ship—nitrogen glaciers and canyons of frozen methane, deep crevasses and strange round holes. When the Osiris REx probe touched down in 2023, Ta and I jumped up and down like crazy people.

Or maybe it was because of my dad, maybe that's where it all came from originally. The Christmas that I was five, my dad had downloaded some free outer-space gaming software and bought cheap flight-simulator controls—a couple of joysticks, some plastic throttles and foot pedals that hooked up to our PC. To me and Ta, it was like piloting the New Horizons probe. We loved it—all three of us loved it—and it was multiplayer, a real family game.

Mo, my dad, when he had the job at Boeing, liked to joke that he worked in the aerospace industry. "Yeah," he'd say, with a serious nod, "I'm in aerospace." Then he'd add, with a smile, "I fly a forklift for Boeing." He'd worked at the Renton plant since we had come over from Honolulu, where my brother and I were born. Growing up in Samoa, forty, fifty years ago, he said, he dreamed of space and dreamed of flight, and he was going to make sure we kids had what we needed to do what we wanted, whatever we wanted to do. And that part was no joke.

Now I work nights at NanoGobblers, a nanotech startup in that big old building at Paine Field, north of Seattle. Twenty years ago, when I was born, it belonged to Boeing and was the biggest building in the world. But that was then, and now it's a walled city of nanotech developers—stacked boxcars full of cubicles and testing labs and people in windowless but air-conditioned rooms. Not exactly the glamorous part of the space industry, but this is the job that is putting me though college. I get an engineering degree, I'll be able to get a real job building the habitats. Maybe even get to go out to them.

Night shifts are quiet. Basically, I just do installation monitoring for nanobot missions: partner with the AI, make sure the bots are working, make sure the incoming data is streaming, check the functionality of the local devices, fix or replace anything that isn't working, answer any questions the AI has. The techs come in at 8:00 a.m., and I go off to class. Sleep? Who needs it?

The other night-shifters and I are the space-tech equivalent of gofers. Low-paid, software-savvy since we were kids, we work nights and weekends in the startups that are competing for piece-work in asteroid mining: nanoware design, testing, and operations management. All nano, all the time. We know we're lucky to have the jobs and the training in this economy. As soon as the development cost is low enough, these jobs will be held by AIs. I'm hoping I'll be promoted by then into another job the AIs can't do yet. It's musical chairs, staying ahead of the AIs.

The air-transportation business fled Everett with the Boeing company and my dad's job went with them. There are no forklifts anymore—no forklifts and no jobs for old guys who graduated from some island high school. Mo got a job in a Samoan sandwich shop. Not great money, but he said that leftover barbecue was an employee benefit that Boeing had never offered. My dad looks on the bright side.

#

Seth fascinates me. He has a brain at least as good as mine, a much better memory, an army of bots to do his bidding, and instant access to all the information in the world, which he keeps with him on a cube the size of your thumb. He talks and he thinks and he makes up his own mind about what he's doing and how to do it. I mean, okay, he's a glorified expert system, but he aces the Turing test, and speaks tech-talk better than I do. I am *almost* extraneous, and if the government allowed Seth to talk directly to a NASA scientist, I'd be out of a job.

Seth powered up fully two months ago, when the probe got to Bennu, and I've gotten to know him pretty well. I get pretty familiar with all the AIs I work with, but he's special: he has mega-meg processing power and a good dose of what they call machine curiosity. I know there are other systems like him in astro-mining and construction, but he's my first curious AI, and more like a pal than a computer.

He teases me by pretending he is various people and characters named Seth. My least favorite was the ten-thousand-year-old entity from *Seth Speaks*, a book that started some kind of a cult fifty years ago or so. That Seth was a bit creepy, frankly. "I will incarnate whether or not you believe that I will." He stopped when I told him it scared me. I would love to know who taught him to do that. I'd take them apart.

Seth learns from experience, so he changes. He's changed a lot in the time I've known him. He's developing a databasey sense of humor, and has just reached the brainy-four-year-old level—or he's malfunctioning in some way, but I can't put my finger on how. Maybe it's a language-sim glitch. I posted a note to NASA about it, but they said it wasn't mission-critical at this point and spindled it.

Seth is always in conversation with other AIs, even while he's in conversation with me. I don't think this is a bad thing: it means he can get a lot of work done at once. Really, only the Saps First people worry about this, and everyone knows they're nuts. The area between the earth and the moon is dotted with AIs and probes and bots and a few people, all trying to find and extract riches from what is mostly empty space.

Here and there are human habitats and redirected chunks of asteroids. Every space-striver in the word has AI-directed machinery up there, trying to lay claim to a rock and pry it apart. Of course not all the AIs talk to one another—some are too old to have the capability, or have no surplus power for nonessential communication, or were designed to function only within narrow parameters. But it's normal now to have the AIs working shipping routes and traffic on the supply lanes without consulting us: we don't worry about collisions anymore. Funny to think there was ever any debate about this.

When he arrived at Bennu, Seth launched a set of explorer-bots. He oversaw them while they searched out amino acids, captured samples, and stored them on Seth for return to Earth-orbit. Now he's deploying our self-replicating nanobots to take Bennu apart, atom by atom.

Bennu comes in close to earth and then swings wide around the sun in a huge ellipse. The closest it will get to us in the next century is 300,000 kilometers, a whole light-second, but closer than the moon. For NASA that is too close for comfort, and they decided to take it apart, as long as they were going there anyway. Memo to self: do not intrude on NASA's comfort zone.

Bennu was probably around before the solar system was created—it's a bit of residue that never got made into a planet and, since it was never subjected to the heat and pressure that form planets, it could hold clues to the whole story of how life developed on Earth. NASA went prospecting there back in the Teens for amino acids and other organic materials, what you might call the ingredients of life—chemicals that, when they come together under the right conditions, form even more complex chemicals that can assemble themselves, kind of like nanobots do. Like nanobots, they're not alive. But, unlike nanobots, they're on their way.

The earlier mission to Bennu, the one that NASA sent out in 2016, didn't even have an AI, but when it returned seven years later, it brought back some very interesting amino acids. So they launched this second mission two years ago, in 2030, with a smart AI to pilot (that's Seth) and better tools to look for more amino acids, molecules of formaldehyde or ammonia, maybe even proteins. Again, the things they're looking for aren't alive, but they're made *from* amino acids, so they're, like, the next step in the recipe. If they find them on Bennu, it could mean that life is older than the solar system. And if life is older than the solar system, it's almost certainly somewhere else. It would mean that we're not alone. After identifying the materials they were looking for, the bots inhaled them and returned to the probe.

Then we began the second phase of the mission. Seth turned loose the slimebots, and they started replicating, using the materials of Bennu itself, mostly carbon and some trace metals. Water frozen in Bennu's rocks provide oxygen and hydrogen to use as fuel. The bots make billions of copies of themselves, and the copies will gobble up the whole asteroid, sorting it molecule by molecule. They'll bag the carbon and ice and fuels, then Seth will put up a light-sail, and sunlight will push the remains of Bennu to the L5 Lagrangian libration point, way out past the moon.

The useful thing about a Lagrangian point is that what you put there stays there, waiting for you to come back. The Consortium is building a commercial storage station there. Mining companies are filling it up with raw materials, for resale to space developers and manufacturers. Nothing, no matter how valuable it seems, is sent back to Earth. "What goes up does not come down," as they say.

#

Once Phase II started, Seth and I were free to just knock back, so we were kidding again about people named Seth. I had eleven other nanobot visual feeds to keep track of, but those feeds are no big deal to keep an eye on—they are mostly small-scale clean-up operations, collecting gold and platinum residue left after nickel and iron mining.

Seth told me he had a video of *The Fly*, a Hollywood chestnut they redo every few decades or so, hoping to get it right. He liked it because the main character is a guy named Seth, who gets turned into a fly in a teleportation accident. (Ha-ha.) We were going to watch just a little bit but ended up watching the whole thing. It was okay, but I'm not a big horror fan.

"Tell me what you think the movie is about," Seth asked.

"I don't know," I said. "The dangers of using uninspected transportation?"

"That is a joke," Seth said. "Its humor resides in the recontextualization of an exotic, even spurious, concept by identifying it with the familiar."

"Bingo," I said.

"But that is not actually what the movie is about. You are not answering my question."

"What do *you* think the movie is about?" I asked.

"It is about me. I am Seth Brundle," he said. "A chimera that is part human and also part something else, something ineffable."

"Is that why you like it?" I asked. This was the strangest joke he'd ever made, and I'd certainly never heard him use the word *ineffable* before. I wondered if it was in the movie.

"I don't know if I *like* it," Seth answered. "I am just collecting information, and when I have enough information, maybe I'll know something. I am not sure I can *like* anything, in your sense. I know that some people like this film and some do not, but that wasn't my question. I asked what you think it is about."

"I don't know. Maybe it's about falling in love and then everything changes and life is horrible?"

"Is that what happens?" asked Seth.

"I don't know," I said. "It's what happened to my friend LaVelle. That's why I have no intention of falling in love."

"Sina, what are you up to?" called Tanisha from her station.

"Just chatting with Seth," I called back.

There were just three of us on the shift, me and Tanisha, and another NSCC frosh named Marcus. That's how it usually is, nights, just a couple of community college students and Tanisha. Marcus caught my eye, rolled his, and I shrugged. My dad says, sometimes the best thing you can do is keep your mouth shut, and this was one of those times, so I went back to monitoring Seth and the other remotes I'm in charge of.

But I felt guilty for farting around, especially for watching a movie, even though Tanisha's pretty mellow about the occasional game of v-chess if things are slow.

I scanned around on Bennu. Everything I could see was covered in that shiny gray fog.

I zipped through visuals on the other bot installations. Everything looked fine, there were no hotspots, just a couple of minor requests from the cubesat repair station. I could take care of those later.

I went back to Seth.

"How come you have access to movies? They're not facts; they're just made up stuff."

"Well, I'm a general-purpose intelligence, and I'm curious." Seth sounded a bit offended. "Everything I learn makes me more adaptable, able to learn more and deal creatively with new situations. So I try to know everything, and I like to try out what I know, test it.

"I know everything that humans know. The sciences, technology, music, the verbal and visual arts. It's all in my database. I know it all at once, and I am good at formulating queries. I am not sure why you watch movies. They seem to take so much of your bandwidth. I don't actually have to watch the movie to know what is in it."

I nodded. Seth is different from the other AIs I've worked with—clearly he had evolved in the two-plus years he'd been traveling to Bennu. I wondered, not for the first time, what he'd been doing all that time, when his communications with Earth were intermittent and he was using only 10 percent of his resources, basically just assessing his course and firing rockets to change it when necessary.

"Right now," Seth continued, "I am imagining being a Brundlefly." That's the creature that Seth Brundle turns into in the movie. It's like half-fly and half-human.

I don't like the Brundlefly idea. Like the weird Seth-Speaks Seth, I am creeped by this Brundlefly Seth. It seemed unhappy. Moody.

Okay, I'm pretty sure AIs can't be moody. Seth did seem to be thinking about his place in the universe, and I'd never seen an AI do that before. It should have been just plain interesting, but it was more than that. It reminded me of a tagline from *The Fly*: "Be afraid. Be very afraid."

I got up to stretch my legs a bit. I moved away from my workstation, and went across the room to where I kept a terrarium. Inside it was Leggs, a rather handsome bright-yellow scrambled-eggs slime mold, and a dog-vomit slime mold named Rover, who was also yellow at the moment. Leggs's special talent is that she pulsates, but she's also good at solving certain kinds of problems. She loves oatmeal, and can find the shortest path in a fairly complicated maze between different piles of it. Also, she's edible, but fortunately for her, she's not that tasty.

I collected Rover when I was a kid, in the woods behind my house. He looks cheery enough now, but at some point he'll turn brown, and then he'll look a lot like dog vomit. He'll dry up and release spores. First time it happened, I mourned him. "Rover is dead!" I said to my dad. "Just wait," he said, and collected the spores. A few months later, he put the spores on some seaweed jelly, and they made a new Rover. "Long live Rover!" he proclaimed.

It's eternal life, being a slime mold. They're simple critters, not quite animal, not quite vegetable. They operate without a larger consciousness to guide them, but they can move, make decisions, find food, and survive to reproduce.

Seth's little bot army, designed by a NanoGobblers programming AI, does the same. Movement—clustering together, spreading out, getting from one place to another—that's the easy part. Making decisions the way slime molds do, as a group of very simple little critters—identifying "food," seizing it, avoiding "poison"—that's the most interesting part.

The bots are based on off-the-shelf kits—self-replicating nano-components that can identify and capture specific atoms and molecules, such as carbon and water. They are programmed with some simple slime-mold functions. They can recognize one another (otherwise they'd eat each other up) and self-assemble into larger systems, and can decide to do so, on their assessment of conditions that could threaten their existence. The question "How do slime molds grow?" offers an approach to network-creation problems, and slime mold reasoning techniques help solve the problem of the shortest distance needed to cover the asteroid and of the number of nanobots needed.

Aside from their personal charms, some slime molds are interesting because of their genetic mechanisms. Rover and his family have been important in unraveling how messenger RNA works, and the AIs referenced that in their designs for the nanobots. It's a weird coincidence—or maybe it's not—but dog-vomit slime molds are also especially rich in introns, enzymes that can fold and splice themselves and are somehow directly involved in the creation of life.

Slime molds like Rover inspired the AIs who created Seth's slime-bots, and they did that in ways that are too complex for us to understand yet. This mission is the first mass deployment of these bots. It's not an accident that it's being done at a distance from Earth.

I'm giving you the short version of my Slime Mold Rap—really, I'm just summarizing here. I could talk about slime molds forever. Don't get me started.

I always feel better after a little time with the slime molds. As I turned to go back to my desk, I glanced over at Rover in his terrarium.

Rover looked very odd. He was still yellow, he was still lumpy, and from this angle he looked like a human head with big globular eyes and wrinkles and a strange mouth. He looked like the Brundlefly. I had the feeling that he was saying, "Help me! Help me!" I moved a little bit away, and he was just Rover again. Whew. I have an over-active imagination, and I guess I shouldn't discuss horror movies with the AIs.

#

It was time to get back to work and see what was up with the messages from the cubesat repair lab. Parts requests, probably. Those old satellites were always breaking down. Shouldn't be a problem.

I thought I'd just take a peek at Seth and his slimebots, before I took care of the cubesat, see how they were doing. I settled in and put my glasses on, and—whoa!—I was struck by the changes on Bennu. It was quite covered in gray goo, and the bots were still replicating.

"Seth, what's going on?" He should have stopped making bots by now.

"Nanobots are replicating efficiently." Yes, that was literally what was going on. There is such a thing as being too polite when talking to a computer.

"You have made enough bots, per the project spec. Stop making bots. Deploy what you have. "

"I have changed the spec. Now we will fabricate the entire asteroid, as I am reasoning that we can ship the material efficiently in the bags as pre-formed bots. I have confirmed this with the L-5 Storage AIs, who anticipate a future need for replicator bots at their site. We have the manufacturing power here to do this, reducing a possible strain on their resources in the future."

Well, that made sense, I thought, but it was creepy to see the gray goo doubling every few minutes. They were going to run out of asteroid pretty fast. "Did you confirm this with NASA and the NG techs?"

"I will send a report for them when I am done, as usual."

"This is a change in plans, Seth. There is no authorization for this. The bots are programmed to function as replicators only for a limited time, and then they deteriorate into components."

"A design flaw. I fixed that."

"It's not a design flaw; it's a safety precaution, a limit on their replicability. The techs need to know this now." Like Rover, the replicator bots would be active for a while, and then would deactivate and reassemble into collectors to harvest the carbon and fuels. Unlike Rover, the replicators would not deactivate into spores. Last thing anybody at NG wants is for gobblers to reproduce forever. That's your gray goo, eating the universe.

"Okay. I will generate a progress report."

"Stop doing it! Wait until you get an okay from Tech."

"I'm sorry, Sina. I cannot implement instructions from you. You are a conduit only. Would you like to watch another movie? I want to hear what you think of *2001*."

Uh-oh. He wasn't wrong. I'm not authorized to input instructions to an AI. I simply don't have that capability. What had he been learning from those damned movies? I yelled over to Tanisha, "Holy cow! Tanisha! I need some help over here!" To Seth, I simply said, "I've already seen *2001*."

Tanisha was at my side immediately. She was unperturbed and simply flipped a quick message to Seth's handlers in Santa Clara. "They'll take care of this. It's not completely unexpected—the curious AIs have a tendency to aggregate information from other systems and implement independent decisions. It's a feature, not a bug. They'll get better at it." And yeah, it seemed to be no huge surprise to the folks in Santa Clara, who promptly walked Seth back.

"They don't seem worried that Seth was going to keep churning out nanobots," I said to Tanisha.

She shook her head. "The gray goo thing? NASA's not dumb. They've got plenty of safeguards, and they can't be countermanded by an AI." She smiled at me. "So cheer up, pumpkin. We're not putting you in charge of keeping the universe from being eaten by nanobots."

"Well, that's a relief," I mumbled.

"But you were trained on this, Sina, and you should have caught it." Tanisha sounded both sympathetic and exasperated. "What happened?"

I was kind of discouraged and plenty embarrassed. "I guess I expected Seth to tell me about decisions he was making."

"Why on earth would you think that? You're supposed to be monitoring what Seth is doing. That's why you're here. Don't go zoning off somewhere."

I figured I'd better head straight for the truth. "Well, we were watching a movie while he was doing this, so why wouldn't he tell me what else he was doing?"

Tanisha looked at me in what I guess was semi-amused disbelief. "Ah. What movie?"

"*The Fly*."

She rolled her eyes, and I was even more embarrassed. "And why were you watching a stupid movie when you should have been working?"

Good question. What was I thinking? "Uh . . . Seth wanted to know what I thought of the movie. He was, y'know, curious about how humans think."

She nodded like she'd just figured something out. "I think we're looking at a little transference here. You're investing Seth with emotions that a computer does not have.

"This is partly my own fault," she added, "for playing along." She shook her head. "I think it's time for the he-or-she game to stop," she said. "No more anthropomorphizing the AI. Also, no more watching movies on the computer. You're not babysitting, you're monitoring system installations. You know that."

Fair enough. I did know that.

"Now get back to work. Think about this a little. If you want to talk to a therapist, I can authorize three half-hour sessions."

#

So I've been thinking. I know I anthropomorphized Seth, but it felt like I was making friends with him. It. Whatever. I could stop. It would probably help if I changed the speaker tone so it was more neutral. I needed to decommission Seth in my brain.

But, you know, humans anthropomorphize everything, given half a chance. Computers, slime molds, people. It makes the world a friendlier place.

Humans are hardwired to anthropomorphize pretty much anything with an apparent behavior. Like when I talk about my bike, right? "She needs her brakes checked." I've even given her a name—I call her Dolores, because, to my sorrow, she always needs some kind of expensive repair.

Am I anthropomorphizing my dog, when I think he loves me, or my cat when she's playing with me? I think that's cross-species communication. Even animals make certain assumptions about the behavior of other animals: this one will eat me, that one will skritch me behind the ears. Is my cat ailuromorphing me to ask for a treat? (Yeah, I looked that up. Wish I spoke Greek.)

Isn't it this kind of communication that makes us conscious beings, and different from rocks? We are aware of ourselves as somehow apart from others, yet somehow a part of some larger entity, some system. So, based on that, is there a difference between us humans going out into the universe and our machines going instead? Are our machines—made of carbon and silicon and other metals—are they rocks that we are throwing? Or are they like cats and dogs and elephants and whales and even (for some of us, anyway) slime molds—creatures with whom we can, mysteriously, emulate understanding?

So here's another question: is it wrong for me to think of programming as an effort to understand others, other beings made of silicon? Is it a sin of pride to believe I'm communicating with a machine?

I don't think so. Our machines, our computers, our AIs are extensions of Earth's community of intelligences: cats, dogs, humans, computers, slime molds, AIs, reaching out into a universe that has lots to teach us about our own origins. So I won't feel bad if it happens that a few nanobots have escaped. They will extend our reach back out into the universe that we came from, and who knows what they will communicate with.

I can govern myself. I'll treat Seth like a computer now and not watch movies at work. And I will try to get out more with real human beings.

And I miss my friend Seth, even though I don't expect he misses me. He's simply not programmed that way. Maybe I do need to talk with that therapist.

"I Did, and I Didn't, and I Won't"
Eileen Gunn interviewed by Terry Bisson

Who are you? Why are you here?

I'm a writer. I write short stories and essays, and this is my third collection. I've also written a few essays about people and ideas and what science fiction is good for. I am probably best known for my story "Stable Strategies for Middle Management," which describes the evolutionary strategies deployed in an unusual corporate ecosystem. From 2002 to 2008, I published and edited the online science-fiction magazine *The Infinite Matrix*. Just before that, for a year or two, from an attic in Brooklyn, I edited the world's largest outdoor recreation website, publishing articles that covered, in heart-stopping detail, everything from hiking in Tierra del Fuego to fishing in a public park off Interstate 5. I also had a career in the advertising and marketing of technology products that began in 1968 and ran in parallel with the development of microcomputers, the commercial internet, and the World Wide Web.

Why am I here? What must I do to justify my existence? When I was younger, the answer to that question was "Write a novel." Now, with the self-knowledge that comes from having matured, I can tell you the answer is "Finish the novel."

Did you wander into science fiction or did you fall?
Familiar story. I started on *Peter Pan* and *Alice in Wonderland* and soon moved on to the hard stuff. I grew up in a rural suburb of Boston in which a tiny drugstore was the only source of *Mad* magazine, science fiction, and the rest of literature. When I was a teenager, I babysat for several people who liked science fiction, and I read my way through their paperbacks, while their kids raised hell. I also read Salinger and Nabokov and my grandmother's Reader's Digest Condensed Books, anything I could get out of the library, laundry lists, etc.

I could have grown up to be a writer of laundry lists, but when I was in college, my creative writing teacher forbade me to write science fiction, and I've been writing it all these years out of sheer orneriness.

You worked at Microsoft early. What was that like?
Ninety-hour weeks, on salary. (A meager salary.) A sense of adventure, because if you saw something that needed doing, you just did it, and suddenly it became part of your job. A modest amount of terror, because the computer industry morphed every three months into something new and strange, and so did all our products and strategies. There was a certain amount of anything-goes.

My favorite cultural moment at Microsoft occurred when I was newly arrived. I passed, in a hallway, a Microsoft tech escorting two customers from IBM. It was an unusually hot summer day, but the IBM fellows were wearing crisp gray suits, white shirts, and ties. The Microsoft guy was wearing dungaree cutoffs, and nothing else. I caught a snatch of what he was saying: "Oh, yes, we have a dress code. You have to."

Was The Infinite Matrix *a luxury car, a pharmaceutical, or the first respectable online SF magazine?*

It was a bit of each: a not-very-respectable luxury pharmaceutical. Its origin was a glorious acid trip, in which I'd been hired by a tech company to create a fabulous online SF magazine and was given the budget to do so. I built it from the ground up during the Web's adolescence, before the adults got involved, with the help of a small raft of programmers and the underground artists Paul Mavrides and Jay Kinney.

It had, over the course of its six years of existence, a daily blog from Bruce Sterling, nonfiction by William Gibson and Howard Waldrop, literary criticism by John Clute, and publishing news and gossip from David Langford. It had new fiction by Ursula Le Guin, Pat Cadigan, Nisi Shawl, Rudy Rucker, Cory Doctorow, Richard Kadrey, Michael Swanwick, and everyone else you've ever heard of. And it had a strange, smart daily feature, "Today in History," by one Terry Bisson, which documented history that hadn't happened yet. He writes it still for *Locus* magazine.

The Infinite Matrix was conceived of and originally funded by Matrix.net because they loved science fiction and thought that all the best UNIX programmers did too. It was rescued by a generous and anonymous donor, and later by auctions and fundraising events. It never learned to provide for itself properly, but it was always free to readers and paid good money to contributors, and when its time was up, it left a lovely corpse: an archive of almost all its content at www.infinitematrix.net.

You often, more than most, collaborate with other writers. How does that work?

Sometimes it works well, and sometimes it doesn't. It works best, I think, when one writer has an idea or a beginning that they don't know what to do with, and another writer sees a way of moving it forward. It can fail when one writer has a vision of what the whole story should be but can't communicate that to the other writer.

The most fun story I ever collaborated on was written with Michael Swanwick, Pat Murphy, and Andy Duncan, and we sketched the story out in advance, leaving room for surprises. In fact, we made surprises mandatory. Or maybe the most fun story was the one I wrote with Rudy Rucker in which, at the end, the two main characters fucked the entire Earth alive. Or maybe it was the one I wrote with Swanwick with the evil elves and the monster that turned into Dick Cheney. Or the one with Leslie What about the high school for psychic teenagers and the criminally insane.

I would never have written any of those stories if left to my own devices.

Why Seattle?

I moved to Seattle for love and economics. It turned out to be a smart move in each case. But sometimes, when I'm driving around the city, my car radio will boom out "This is KUOW, Seattle," and I'll think, "Seattle? What am I doing in Seattle?"

What is Ted Chiang really like?

I could tell you, Terry, but if I did I'd have to exile you to a parallel universe.

What music do you listen to most often?
I asked my iTunes app, and it replied that the music I listen to most often is reggae by the Abyssinians, followed closely by accordionist Adam Trehan, a Cajun musician who recorded four sides for Columbia in 1928 and then left music forever. I think iTunes must be wrong about this. I have long been a fan of the Holy Modal Rounders, the Fugs, the Clamtones, the Pogues, Delta blues, and Elizabethan lute music, but the musician I listen to most often right now is probably singer/songwriter Warren Zevon, who's been dead for nearly twenty years and to whom I rarely listened when he was alive.

I used to play guitar and lute, so I listen to a lot of guitar and lute music. I can't write while listening to music, however, so I have had to make hard choices.

Jeopardy question: I provide the answer, you come up with the question. *Originality not a requirement.*
Okay, Terry, here's the question: What is reality?

You started out as a copywriter (so did I). Was that a lucky break or a hitch?
Both. It was a lucky break because my first real copywriting job was at a small agency run by funny, talented lefties who did clever campaigns for high-tech clients. They taught me how to understand

subjects I'd never studied and how to work with capitalists without becoming one.

Writing ads was a hitch in my fiction career because I got really good at short, snappy sentences and never mastered the long, loopingly graceful writing you need to write novels. Twitter is my ideal length, and it's all advertising's fault.

One sentence on each, please: John Clute, Lord Buckley, Jean Auel.
I have always liked Jean Auel, because her name is pronounced Gene Owl, and I like owls and genes. I have always wondered how Lord Buckley, an American, came to be a vassal of the King. It's been nearly thirty years, but I'm still grateful to John Clute for sitting me down in his favorite chair, handing me a cup of hot black coffee, and playing directly into my jet-lagged brain the newly released track of Bob Dylan singing "Blind Willie McTell."

What kind of car do you drive? It seems I ask this of everyone.
Right now? A copper-colored 2015 Fiat 500. Why?

If you could take Oscar Wilde out for a drink in Seattle, where would you go? What would you order?
Either Canlis, the most expensive restaurant in the city, or one of the rougher bars down by the waterfront, if any of them are still there. I'd let him make the call. I would order Death in the Afternoon, a cocktail invented, they say, by Ernest Hemingway, consisting of a decent iced champagne poured over a shot of absinthe until it turns the color of a mossy pearl.

If Clarion and WisCon had a child, who would it be?
Quvenzhané Wallis, both the actress and her brave, independent character in *Beasts of the Southern Wild*.

The Clarion and Clarion West workshops, held for aspiring writers of speculative fiction, are about individuals venturing out into the unknown, often at an early age and with no clear destination. I attended the Clarion Workshop in 1976, and it improved both my fiction and my reality. I later joined the board of the Clarion West workshop, a similar six-week convocation, which exists to empower women and BIPOC+LGBTQ writers of speculative fiction, and I occasionally teach a week.

WisCon is an annual convention, held in May. It celebrates and furthers speculative fiction that reflects the richness and diversity of the human imagination. I have attended it frequently over the past thirty years, as its interests moved from feminism to issues of race and gender and cultural appropriation. In addition to being about politics and books, WisCon is about diligently examining who you are, what you mean, and how you affect others. Sometimes that's fun and sometimes it's threatening to one's self-esteem, but it's always been worth the effort. As I write this, WisCon has been in pandemic hiatus for the past two years, but I expect it to reopen stronger than ever. Check it out.

What poetry do you read for fun?
All poetry, really. Never had a job in which I was obliged to read poetry.

The book of poetry that I've had the most fun with lately is *Dictator*, by the Oulipian poet Philip Terry, which is a re-creation of the Epic of Gilgamesh using the 1,500-word vocabulary of Globish, a sort of pidgin created for use in business communications by non-native English speakers. Oulipian writers use constraints on their writing to force themselves into new ways of thinking and expressing their thoughts. *Dictator* is a wondrous work that transcends the limits of time and translation: it channels the imagined voice and psyche of a Bronze Age storyteller in ways that conventional translations do not. Also, it makes me laugh out loud and demand that people listen to me read especially wonderful passages. The one in which the trapper is explaining to the harlot how to seduce Enkidu is my favorite.

I am also very much drawn to the poems of JT Stewart, a remarkable poet and teacher, a Black woman who has had a strong presence in the Seattle poetry and literary scenes over the past forty years. Her poems are very immediate, grounded in the now, even when they speak in the voices of people who died centuries ago. My partner, the book designer John D. Berry, is working with JT to put together *Our Bones Sing of Salt*, a collection of all her published poems.

There are lots more, but that's enough. Philip Terry and JT Stewart are both visceral poets: their poems engage with a rush of sound and meaning. That is pure poetry.

You attended a Catholic college. How come?
I made a deal with God: I would attend eight years of Catholic schooling, and if I still didn't believe in Him at the end of it, I wouldn't have to believe and would not be expected to repent on my death bed. I did, and I didn't, and I won't, and I am not planning to.

What do you read for pleasure these days?

The book that has given me the most delight in the past month is the newly released collection of comic strips by Shari Flenniken, *Trots and Bonnie*. First published in the *National Lampoon* in the 1970s and '80s, they are exquisitely inked with an elegant Art Deco aesthetic and an incongruously filthy sense of the ridiculous.

What role does humor play in SF—feature, bug, ornament?

Terry, that's like asking what role garlic plays in dinner. Humor is hard to get a handle on, because it's entirely subjective: what's funny to me is not necessarily funny to you. But I know from your writing that what's funny to *you* is pretty damn funny to me.

What is the Difference Dictionary?

The Difference Dictionary is Dr. Gunn's Patented History Restorer, intended for SF readers who have had their understanding of the nineteenth century scrambled by William Gibson and Bruce Sterling's novel *The Difference Engine*. Properly administered, the Dictionary will restore the hairy details of the history of our time stub, and the hapless reader will no longer think of Lord Bryon as a radical politician, Texas as an independent country, and computers as giant clockworks made of rosewood and brass. I wrote the dictionary in 1990 as a sort of review of the novel, and in 1997, while learning to code in HTML, I coded it and posted it on the Web. A few hours later, it was declared Cool Site of the Day, I guess because it was sort of a single-sourced Wikipedia, but Wikipedia didn't exist yet. You can find its dry bones (untouched for a decade or more) at eileengunn.com/difference-dictionary.

Why isn't science fiction taken seriously as literature?

It's true that the marketing category known as science fiction is often not taken seriously, but what marketing category is? Romance novels? Best sellers? Big fat fantasy novels? Jane Austen wrote romance novels. Charles Dickens wrote best sellers. Mary Shelley wrote science fiction. I don't think that the writer or reader has to transcend genre for a book to be taken seriously—I think the academy has to.

Ever fish?

I fished when I was a kid. Another kid taught me to fish. I had a reel and line and had been jumping around from rock to rock, wondering what to do. He caught a grasshopper, baited the hook, told me where he'd recently seen a legal-sized trout, waited with me, and gave pointers on how to drag the line a bit. After I hooked the fish, he told me how to land it, then he killed it quickly so it wouldn't suffer and showed me how to scale, gut, and clean it. Then we walked back to the campsite, and I told my mother, "I caught a fish!" which was certainly an exaggeration and may in fact have been an actual injustice.

Transitions

My first reaction when I saw the future? All that water. As the plane descended out of the clouds, it looked like the whole southern end of San Francisco Bay had been inundated: the flood-walls, all the pumps and dikes and berms, they were like fortifications. The runways stuck up like piers, in a huge shallow lagoon. I thought, wow, what happened here while I was gone? I had been in Shanghai for a conference on robotics and then to Tokyo for a private demo of some amazingly capable service robots, and I hadn't been paying a lot of attention to the dramas that were playing out in the US in the summer of 2017—political, meteorological, what-have-you. I was busy.

So my first peep at the future was a riot of misconception: I thought the flood-control walls and the raised runways—a billion-dollar, decade-long engineering project—were a temporary response to some humongous Bay Area rainstorm. Silly me: maybe I needed glasses.

After we landed, we were interrogated by people in uniform, though the uniform of what, I couldn't determine. They told us we'd gone twenty years off-course, and they wanted to know how. I didn't believe what they were saying at first: it seemed like a prank or like some sci-fi movie plot. I wondered if it had anything to do with military applications for the robots I'd just seen demonstrated. I'd signed NDAs, so they were barking up the wrong tree there, I thought.

We spent a couple hours with these guys, who I figured were either spies or doctors or both. They gave us physical exams, and then each of us got a bracelet like a Fitbit to wear. They said it would monitor our health and also keep track of where we are, like cell phones did. They said we couldn't take them off, and they were right: I tried.

Then we were led through SFO, a group of stunned and exhausted people who had just spent nine hours on a plane and had missed their destination by two decades. We were totally in shock and still not ready to believe what the people in the avant-garde lab coats were telling us, that we had slipped through some crack in the space-time continuum. The crowds moving through the International Terminal—a conspicuously airy space with huge fans—were much browner and blacker than the crowds I'd left behind just a week (and two decades) earlier. There were still white people—light-skinned people, anyway—but the balance had changed. More people looked like me than didn't.

When I was younger, I took a vacation trip to West Africa. When I disembarked in Lagos, I was momentarily overwhelmed to see all those Black people and to think that all over the city, all over the country, all over the whole continent, they were just going about their business, living their lives, getting in one another's way, and they were all Black, as Black as I was, and more. I looked at the crowds, and then I laughed. Was I surprised at seeing so many Black people in

Africa? It wasn't surprise, though: it was amazement. And in that way, I was, just then, similarly amazed, in America. That was the moment I felt that I really *was* someplace different from where I'd started, that some fundamental change had taken place.

A couple days later, after many hours of talking with the spy/doctors, and no longer skeptical of what they told us, the few of us who had been en route to DC were guided nervously onto a private plane, and two hours later we arrived at Obama/Dulles without further misadventure. We were hurried through the old Eero Saarinen terminal, an engineering marvel in its time but now, at seventy-five, looking a bit dog-eared. I was gawking a bit at the people we passed. They seemed to be mostly businesspeople, but they too were wearing the most outlandish clothes. Some folks showed a lot more skin than was usual for DC, and others were wearing loose robes, Arab-style, with writhing iridescent patterns on them. Disturbing.

When I went outside, the air was heavy with humidity, and the temperature was like a building on fire. It made July in Tokyo seem like April in Bar Harbor. There were outlets spraying chilled air every few meters, and we were quickly moved to buses and whisked off to Langley, Virginia, for further examination and a couple days of reality therapy: a quick update on where we were, and when. When they were done with me, they said, they would inform my family I was alive, and turn me over to them. Up until then, apparently, even in San Francisco, we had been the secret guests of the spy/doctors of Langley, Virginia. Wham-bam-thank-you-ma'am.

Over the course of the next three days, I came up to speed. I began to understand what had happened in the past twenty years.

The US privatized, then re-org'ed and distributed itself into eight groups—nine if you include Texas, which had always been a group all by itself. In DC, now Columbia, the government office buildings, protected against the rising water by dikes, were picked up for pennies on the dollar by investors from around the globe. These oligarchs, a descriptor they prefer to "mobster," have retooled much of the world economy to their benefit, but they still permit niches in which ordinary people can survive and prosper, and Columbia is one of them. Langley seems to be some kind of independent government: its reach is clearly beyond the local groups.

The Troubles, the fractured politics of the past two decades, endlessly varied and frankly surreal, are beyond my immediate understanding, and I will leave them alone. Since the breakup, every former state has its own rules and regulations, and it is enough for me to understand that I do not understand. At least I know which states to avoid, both as a Black person and as a woman.

I wrapped my head around what had happened and realized I could never go back to where I came from. In Columbia (former District of) in 2037, there were companies who wanted to study me and my co-passengers and would pay us a living wage to allow it. We would be lab rats in an effort to understand the nature of time—and to see if it could be controlled. They seemed to think that there was hyperspace dust clinging to us, and if they observed us long enough, some of it would rub off on them. I didn't want to be a lab rat, and it was clear that I had to develop a few options for my own future.

For me, the most exciting change was not a surprise; it was something humans had dreamed of for thousands of years. We were colonizing the Moon, and despite the Troubles, we were on schedule. Privately owned conglomerates from India and Malaysia had taken over where governments had left off, building orbiting factories to manufacture electronics components and establishing several Moon bases for future development. Near-earth asteroids were now routinely captured and mined for fuel and volatiles not available on the Moon. There was even talk of a Mars mission, planned by NASA over thirty years before. Teams were being assembled. Teams were actively being recruited for missions in both areas, and the standing nerd joke was "The Moon needs engineers, but Mars needs women!"

It was definitely an advantage, in this situation, to be an engineer. Even though my skills were now laughably out of date, I had the intellectual tools to analyze the situation dispassionately, identify its unique problems, and come up with a strategy.

I like to look at the world in terms of Venn diagrams. I belong to a number of intersecting sets—for example, I'm Black, I'm a woman, I'm an engineer. This gives me something in common with other members of these sets and gives me tools for communicating with them. Sometimes it gives me an obligation of group solidarity, but it also might set me apart in certain ways, in terms of characteristics we do not have in common. The number of Black engineers, in 2017, was relatively small, and the number of engineers who are both Black and women was infinitesimal. But the situation was very different in 2037, and chances were good that in a workplace on the Moon I would not be particularly lonely.

The time-jump had put me in an additional set, though. I call it the set of the Invisible Aliens, the people who look like members of a group, but behave according to different rules. The group notices this in a subliminal way, and it leads to awkward social situations. In my case, I had not mastered the 2037 rubrics for social interaction: the appropriate distances, greetings, responses, etc. I'd experienced a similar social learning curve as a nerdy kid and a clueless young woman—too close, too distant; too casual, too formal; too loud, too reserved. So I did what had worked for me before: I followed the cues that other people offered about our status-relationship. I got some of the weird clothing, which had some kind of heat-shield in it, and I went out in public and talked to strangers. I practiced until I passed as normal, and then I figured I was ready, with the help of the spy/doctors, to come out to my family. Looking for a job would come later.

I needed to restore the continuity of my relationships: my son (no longer a child), my husband (now someone else's husband as well), my mom and dad, who divorced when I was a kid. My family was the least predictable part of my life now, the area over which I had the least control. What would they do? How would they act? To them I had been dead for twenty years, and to me, they would not be the family I knew. I had to get to know the people that they had become. I am not a person who is comfortable with strangers. It worried me.

It turned out that our plane was not the first that had made some kind of a transition and showed up in the future. Langley had an entire rubric for re-inserting us into our lives.

The spy/doctor said it would be best if they spoke to my family members without me there. "Give them a couple days," she said. "Let them get used to the idea." She arranged everything. She decided who

I'd see first: my son, Malcolm. "He's the one with the most riding on this," she said.

What about me? I thought. But I didn't say anything.

They had rooms reserved for these meetings in Langley, tastefully appointed with drapes and upholstery in the great vibrating patterns that decorated people's clothing. "It's calming," the spy/doctor said. Right.

Meeting with my son was a strange combination of emotions—joy at what he'd turned into, a grown-up, a scientist, a husband and father. He and his partners had two kids and another on the way. The Langley folks showed me photos of them all in advance, with his permission. His husband and wife looked comfortable and happy and the kids (my grandkids!) looked suitably mischievous.

Still, when he entered the room, tall and filled out, looking a lot like his dad, I was struck by the sum of everything he was, and how little I knew of it. I felt a great loss, the loss of all the time he had been evolving into who he was. I felt so left out of his life—he'd turned into an adult without my help. But to him, I was exactly the mother he remembered, back from the dead. He was filled with tearful joy to see me, but my emotions were confused. I didn't know how to love this almost-stranger. I'm sure my feelings will resolve into the affection he deserves, but to me, my son is only seven.

The most distressing thing about meeting with Malcolm was that I didn't get any of his jokes. I could tell they were jokes, we're a funny family, or we were. But none of them meant anything to me. Back in 2017, I was hip to the snarky political people on Twitter and BET, and even Stephen Colbert. At seven, Malcolm loved Stephen Colbert, though I think most of the jokes went over his head. In 2037, they were all long gone, as was Twitter for that matter, and I would have to rebuild.

He brought his partners and the kids, and I can see him in his boys. I can play with them with their toys and hear their adventures and learn the new vocabulary of today's children. Maybe they will fill that unfillable hole inside me, where my sweet, vulnerable son used to be.

The meeting with Leon, my husband, my *former* husband, went a bit better from my point of view, but this time it was he who was off-balance. He looked like himself, for one thing, just a bit more weathered, and I don't mean that in a bad way. I was so happy to see him. We'd been apart for weeks, to my mind. I wanted to hold onto him and have him comfort me, after all I'd been through. But that clearly made him very uneasy.

"Um . . ." He pulled back a little. "I brought my wife, Alika. She's waiting outside." He sat down in one of the side chairs.

"I'm sorry," he said. "I'm still astonished. Who ever heard of such a thing?"

"It's all right, honey," I said. "But you gotta understand that to me, you're my husband, who I haven't seen in two weeks, and I missed you."

"Should I bring Alika in, now?"

Well, that wasn't very flattering. Men. "Relax, tiger, I'm not going to jump your bones. Let's just talk a little bit first." I smiled at him, just a little wistfully.

Wistfully! At my own husband!

He was still wary, but he smiled back cautiously, just like my husband when he knows he's out on thin ice. "We been married eighteen years, me and Alika," he said. "Twice as long as you and me were."

Yeah, I was jealous of this Alika. She must be hell on wheels, if he's that worried about me being demonstrative. Nah, this was too awkward. If I was going to play second fiddle to the woman, she might as well come in. Let's clear the air . . .

"Oh, for Pete's sake. Go get her. Bring her in."

His face lit up. "She's been so good for me and Malcolm. Mal suffered so much with the loss of his mama." He caught himself. "With *your* loss." He looked confused.

I made an it's-okay gesture. Calm down, Leon, I thought. His face always showed me exactly what he was thinking.

He stood up and moved towards the door. "She was a mother to Malcolm through his teen years, during the Troubles, when chemical and electronic mods were so tempting to young people."

That just about stabbed me in the heart, but I tried not to show it. I was doubly jealous, but I was glad to learn that she was there for my boy, that he had someone watching out for him.

Leon turned back towards me. "And she brought me to Jesus," he said. "And it made all the difference. I was in such despair."

I am not a religious person, Leon knew that, but I have no problem with people who keep their religion to themselves. As so far he had, and we'd just see about Alika. "Well, go get her, for pity's sake," I said. "I wouldn't have wanted you and Mal to have spent the last two decades in despair." I hadn't thought about that before blurting it out, but having said it, I realized it was true. That would have been an awful thing to have happen.

Leon came back in a few seconds, leading a short, plump, almost grandmotherly woman by the hand. Her hair was braided and wrapped in a crown around her head. "Alika," he said, "this is Shannay."

Not quite the Dragon Lady I had envisioned. She must be twenty years older than me, I thought. And Leon would be sixty-two this year. I could see their eighteen years together on their faces and on the way they held hands. Alika reached over with her free hand and took mine, and squeezed it gently. "Hello, my dear," she said. "Welcome back."

"Thank you," I replied. "Thank you so much for everything." I wanted to make it clear from the beginning that I was indebted to her, and I knew it.

The three of us talked for a couple of hours, and in the course of our conversation, I realized that Leon looked more like his father than himself. Such a difference twenty years makes. This was not my husband. This was not the man who kissed me goodbye when I left for China and Japan, just a couple weeks ago. I do miss my husband, but this Leon is not him. My son, however, is hers too.

After those two fraught days, the meeting with my parents went really well. Of course my parents were amazed and delighted at my return, and we had a happy reunion, even though they don't spend much time together anymore. We went out for barbecue, at my dad's new favorite place. He said our old favorite closed ten years ago, when the southeast DC flooded, and the building had to come down. The food was good at the new place, though the sides are all different and confusing—sambal in *everything*. I liked the old place better, where we always went when I was a kid. In fact, I was there just last month, before I went to Japan.

My folks are in their late seventies, and, yeah, they look old to me. I would never have guessed that they'd be in such great shape, though. They're like people in their forties. I mean, like people used to be in their forties. Old folks just don't get old as fast they used to, and young people don't either.

That wrist-monitor the spy/doctors gave me—they both have something like it, and they wear it all the time. "It keeps track of our medical well-being," my dad said, like right out of an ad. It can even administer medication if it decides that's needed. When I showed them I had one, they were impressed. "CIA," my dad said. "That's a really nice one: it'll keep you safe as well as healthy. We've got the best ones we can afford, but even a Catholic Charities monitor will keep you going."

All in all, a better meeting than the first two. They're still my parents, and they still treat me like a kid, even though I'm all growed up. Just my brother and sister to go, but they live up north. I'll call after my mom breaks the news to them.

It had been a long week, emotionally exhausting, but it made one thing clear: the people I used to have lives with, they now had lives without me. That's the thing about being dead: people move on. I wasn't actually necessary anymore.

So now I'm looking for a job, and I'm seeing robots everywhere. Robots from companies in India and Greater California are mining captured asteroids for carbon and water. Robots from Shanghai are building yet another manufacturing operation out beyond the Moon. Robots have landed on Mars and are assembling human habitats there. They won't be luxurious, but there will be condos already built when we arrive.

There really *are* opportunities on the outer planets—or in the asteroid belt, at least. The robots have gotten there first, but I can catch up. I'm sure that, if I have to, I can get a robot to teach me what I need to know.

Joanna Russ Has Your Back

"She told often unpalatable truths in tales that
were, as pure story, a joy to read."
—John Clute

Joanna Russ, best known as the author of the groundbreaking
science-fiction novel *The Female Man* and a nonfiction guide for
the oppressed, *How to Suppress Women's Writing*, wrote pretty much
anything she wanted to: science fiction, sword and sorcery, fantasy,
literary fiction, polemics and diatribes, critiques and reviews, and her
brilliant, brief account of the ways women writers have, through history, been disappeared from the canon. A feminist at a time when
feminism was even more suspect than it is today, a lesbian in a society
that feared lesbians, she fought the world on her own terms, and the
world listened, said "What the *fuck*?" and fought back.

Joanna's stories and essays addressed issues of gender and politics,
sometimes with humor, sometimes with anger, and always with a
fiery sense of setting things right. Her first published story was the
short, slyly humorous "Innocence," which appeared in the Cornell
literary magazine in 1955, when she was eighteen. The protagonist
of the story is self-described as "dark as a mole," but never by gender,

and early reviewers assumed both characters were male, because in those days science-fiction stories contained few active females. To twenty-first-century eyes, it is obviously the story of a small, dark woman being condescended to by a big, gorgeous blond guy, and she's stringing him along with a fantastic tale.

When Joanna started selling stories professionally a few years later, her stories continued to challenge conventional readers: the muscular heroes were women, they wielded their own weapons, and, occasionally, they lived their lives entirely separate from the world of men. *The Female Man* compares the lives of four women living in parallel worlds and examines the compromises and mistakes they make when trying to deal with issues of gender. It was written nearly fifty years ago, and the issues it raises are still unresolved.

Joanna's stories and novels were called angry, although what they really were was direct. She was not the first feminist or the first lesbian to write science fiction, not by a long shot, but she was one who attracted the most hostility. Although she focused on the overt oppression of women that had overshadowed her life and career, Joanna recognized and acknowledged that Black people and people of color, gay and lesbian people, and others experience multiple discriminations—the cumulative force of which professor Kimberlé Crenshaw, a few years later, defined as intersectionality.

Descriptions of Joanna's work often focus on the message, rather than on the experience of reading her prose, which is smart, elegant, and often funny, as she indicates the difference between what is and what should be. And it is, as John Clute says, a joy to read. When writing this essay, I sat down with a handful of her books to refresh my memory, and I am again entranced by the way she writes.

Joanna Russ was one of my instructors at the Clarion Writers Workshop in 1976; she became a friend after I moved to Seattle in 1977. She seemed to me, in her writing and in her life, always to be pushing back with fierceness and wit against the weapons—condescension and denial—that were and still are used to keep brilliant women in their place. Her book *How to Suppress Women's Writing* is a short, clever discussion of the arguments that have been used to silence women and other marginalized groups of people since the beginning of Western literature. It offers writers and artists a detailed account of the techniques used to silence them, deny them agency, to make them seem smaller than they actually are, and make them doubt their capabilities and accomplishments. Born from experience, not from theory, and supported by the historical record, it is a tool that women, people of color, and people who are outside the majority's gender orientation can use to understand and defend against the common attacks that are leveraged against them. "She didn't write it." "She wrote it, but she shouldn't have." "She wrote it, but she isn't really an artist and it isn't really art."

In the mid-1980s, after nearly thirty years of publishing stories, essays, and critiques, and burdened by illness and depression, Joanna's pace slackened. Her last significant short story was first published in 1982. *How to Suppress Women's Writing* came out in 1983. She continued to write essays occasionally, but her books that came out after 1985 were collections of previously published essays and stories. She wrote letters and the occasional short essay, she may have polished or revised her work for reprinting, and she continued to teach and inspire students at the University of Washington. She seemed, in the years that I knew her best, to be fighting hard against a writing block, and to be struggling with the interrelated problems of pain control and depression.

After she left Seattle for Tucson in 1994, I corresponded with her a bit and spoke with her on the phone a few times. The last time I spoke to her, in 2010, she seemed genuinely happy. She was reading and talking, and was actually cheerful. What she wasn't doing was writing: I asked her, and she said no. She said she didn't mind: it was okay. She wanted to read lots of books and talk on the phone about them. "I might not write back, but I like to talk on the phone," she said. I was glad she was happy, but as someone who writes slowly and with an effort, I was baffled by Joanna's peaceful acceptance of not being able to write. Such a brilliant writer: wasn't it worth all the effort, all the frustration, when the results were superb?

Joanna died in Tucson in 2011, and a few months later, at WisCon, the feminist science-fiction convention, I was invited to say a few words in remembrance of her. I was to speak after writer/editor L. Timmel Duchamp, a friend of Joanna's and mine. Timmi gave a deeply moving eulogy. She spoke of Joanna's compelling presence and incisive wit, of her place in the history of science fiction as a writer, a critic, and a feminist, and of her decades-long struggle with physical pain and depression.

Much of what Timmi said I already knew, and I welcomed her account. Joanna was quite tall, a bit gangly, and not enormously well socialized. She could be abrupt, and she said what she thought, without varnish. She had a huge intellect, and when she was entranced by a topic, she pursued it single-mindedly. She graduated from the Bronx High School of Science in 1953, where she was a Westinghouse Science Scholar, one of the ten top high school science students in the entire United States.

In short, Joanna was a geek. A real geek, the kind who becomes a successful scientist or engineer. She was a young, female geek in 1953, which was an especially difficult time to be a female geek. Earlier, women scientists were anomalies, weirdos. But in the postwar years, when Rosie the Riveter was supposed to be taking off her kerchief and overalls and returning to motherhood and civilian life, they were usurpers, taking the jobs that rightfully belonged to men. There was a lot of pressure on them to get back—if not back to the kitchen, then at least back to the liberal arts—and leave science and engineering to the men.

So Joanna Russ, a Westinghouse Science Scholar, admitted to Cornell University at age sixteen, was discouraged by faculty there from going into science and was placed in the English department. She arrived with an enormous amount of talent, and she had an excellent education at Cornell and Yale, but she might have, if she had followed her inclination, become a great scientist. She came to literature as a second choice.

When Timmi finished her superb, deeply felt eulogy, I was a bit at a loss. She had covered everything I was going to say and more. However, while listening to her and thinking about Joanna, I had had a realization about Joanna's creative life and the possible origins of Joanna's silence for the past quarter-century, something that had been hidden from me by the sheer size of Joanna's personality: her feistiness, her talent, and her accomplishments. Perhaps *How to Suppress Women's Writing* was not the objective, well-observed, gallantly helpful historical research I had always taken it for. Perhaps that book was driven by Joanna's personal experience of how her own aspirations had been cut short. And perhaps it derived as well from her own power struggles with other women science-fiction writers. Back in the day, it seems, there was room in science fiction for only one woman at a time.

Those thoughts brought to my mind Tillie Olsen's remarkable book *Silences*, which, among many other things, connects the dots between having writer's block and being a woman. It considers the lives of writers—both men and women—who do not write for some portion of their lives. Maybe they raise children or support a family. Maybe they have been silenced by critics or political oppression or the bland inhibition of living in a world that simply doesn't care about what they do. Whatever the reason, they don't write. Olsen makes the act of a writer not writing seem less a character flaw and more a reasonable response to adverse conditions. Perhaps, I thought, Joanna's silence was just that: a silence, not a block. A well-earned rest.

Perhaps Joanna, who had been forced out of her chosen lifework in the sciences, had leveraged her estimable writing and reasoning skills to examine her own suppression, and that was the remainder of what she had to say to the world. She had left us a clear list of the methods of the patriarchy, and had earned a right to her silence and to the contentment that seemed to come to her late in life.

Although *How to Suppress Women's Writing* is heading for its fortieth birthday, the techniques of suppression that it details are still widely practiced. Whatever your intersectionalities, you may want to consult it in the interest of your own defense.

Take a look at her novels as well. Forty years later, Joanna Russ still has your back.

Into the Wild with Carol Emshwiller

"Carol Emshwiller's stories, and David Bunch's, were a sort
of bridge for me, whereby I could walk back and forth from
sci-fi to Wm. Burroughs and the other Beat/avant-garde stuff I
discovered around thirteen years of age. Over in Burroughs et
al., I could never figure out what the territory was for, whereas
I knew that genre sf was for the repeated induction of a certain
containable frisson. Her stories spanned the divide for me
before the New Worlds crew started building pleasure barges."
—William Gibson[*]

SO. WILLIAM GIBSON CUT his metaphoric teeth on Carol Emshwiller's
stories. I can't think of a flintier substance. Emshwiller was a delicate-
looking woman with the cheekbones of a sci-fi heroine machine-
gunning a nest of Martian invaders, and she wrote stories that took
no prisoners.

My favorite of Carol's stories, the one of which I am most in
awe, is "Acceptance Speech," a tale of the literary apprenticeship of

---

[*]   From private correspondence, used with permission.

a human being to a celebrated alien poet in an alien society, perhaps on another planet. The apprenticeship is cruel and peculiar: the protagonist is forced to compose poetry in a language he doesn't speak, governed by a prosody he doesn't understand. He is beaten and humiliated by his teacher when he gets anything wrong. He submits, he learns. Eventually he dominates. When I heard her read it, in a bar full of writers in New York City, it made my hair stand on end.

Emshwiller stories should come with warning labels: Do not operate heavy machinery while reading these stories. Avoid psychedelics when reading an Emshwiller story. Do not stay up all night, reading story after story by flashlight, under the covers, because you could find yourself with an inexplicable desire to drive your heavy machine off-road into the mountains, flashing all your turn signals and violating the social contract. You could permanently alter your brain chemistry, so that you are incapable of ignoring your perfectly reasonable impulse to move into a stranger's house and break him or her to your will. Deprived of sleep, myopic, and running on two D batteries, you could become convinced that subverting the natural order is not only an option, but a mandate.

Were Emshwiller's stories always subversive? When I asked her, she said no, but how can we trust this woman? All those unreliable narrators . . . I did a spot check on a few stories—well, maybe more than a few: they're pretty much irresistible, and a quick spot check turns into several lost hours, sometimes days, in which reality has become malleable . . .

Her earliest works, "a hundred stories that never sold," are lost in the mists of time, but her first published stories, from the 1950s, are witty satires of American domesticity. Her many stories from the mid-1960s and early '70s—funny, audacious, superbly imaginative, and in complete control of the material—would subvert a Stepford wife. Many of them document bizarre skirmishes in the battle of the sexes, no quarter given and none taken. Something similar could be said of her first novel, *Carmen Dog* (1990)—the hapless but determined Pooch, evolving from dog to woman, seizes control from her master, but, as Carol pointed out to me, she still sleeps on the doormat.

After 1990, Carol's stories took an evolutionary turn, one of those sudden, life-related leaps that sometimes punctuate the work of an artist. Her husband, the artist and filmmaker Ed Emshwiller, died that year. Carol says, "My whole reason for writing changed for a while after my husband died. I needed people to live with, I needed someone to push against . . . As I began writing my western, *Ledoyt*, I didn't feel lonely at all. I was living with my characters more intimately than I ever had before in my whole writing life."

Ledoyt was published in 1995, and its sequel, *Leaping Man Hill*, in 1999. In these books, the ironic distance between Carol and her characters, so evident in her previous stories, is compressed. The tone of these novels is congruent with the earlier stories—Carol's unique writing voice is still there—but the reader finds herself participating more, feeling the character's emotions rather than observing them. *Report to the Men's Club and Other Stories*, though published in 2002, is not so much a document of Carol's continued evolution as a window on the process: it includes previously uncollected stories from the 1970s and '80s, as well as work from the

1990s and after. All of it is wonderful and startling, all of it is worth reading and rereading.

In her novel *The Mount* (2002), she integrates this close-in characterization with a science-fiction plot, creating for the reader a disorientingly intimate journey into a bizarre and creepily familiar relationship. In the first chapter, a creature riding on a human's shoulders makes clear, in the gentlest of tones, how proud it is of the handsome domesticated beast it rides, how generous it has been to him, and how discriminating it is in the disciplinary use of a "pole," which is all the scarier because its mechanism is left undescribed.

Emshwiller published brilliant stories for well over half a century and was a more prolific writer in her eighties than many writers are over their entire lives. These stories, too, are different from her earlier works: more intent, less playful; sparer, more essential. Without sacrificing subtlety, they are more direct. Although Carol did not completely leave behind the battle of the sexes, her later stories detail defections and private truces in a larger war: men and women engaged in hand-to-hand combat with life itself.

During the first decade of the current century, several of my writer friends and I would visit Carol at her summer home in the Owens Valley of California, where she lived and hiked and wrote in a comfortably shabby single-wide trailer a few miles south of Bishop. We hiked with her in the mountains and in spectacular high-desert terrain, where the rain evaporates before it hits the ground. We lay on the driveway at night staring into the glorious Milky Way, as the International Space Station moved silently overhead. And we workshopped our stories. At first we took a conventional workshop approach, in which we lounged about in the trailer, read one another's stories, then sat at the picnic table in the swept-dirt front yard and commented on them, each of us taking our turn. Over a few years, we all relaxed, to a point where we'd just tell one another the story while sitting around a campfire, which is actually a great way to discover the holes in a story you're working on.

When we visited, Carol, by then in her eighties, casually led us to places that I would never have gone alone: across a river on a fallen tree, over the John Muir Trail in a hailstorm, up onto an obsidian dome in the desert . . . At one point, switchbacking up a steep, little-used trail to a wildflower meadow a few thousand feet above the valley floor, my friend Pat and I looked down the hillside and saw that Carol, a tiny, white-haired, eighty-seven-year-old woman alone on the trail below us, was being approached by a group of maybe eight people sitting uncomfortably on horseback, led by a professional guide. The guide said something to her, she replied, and the riders looked at her dubiously, then moved on along a lower trail. What the hell? Were they asking directions? When she caught up to us, I said, "What did they say to you?" She looked bemused. "They said, 'How did you *get* here?'" "I walked," she said, and they rode away uncertainly on their horses.

Across the valley from where Carol lived is the Ancient Bristlecone Pine Forest, home to the earth's oldest living inhabitants, trees that have survived for thousands of years in a climate so inhospitable that they have no predators or competition, growing so slowly that they become their own impermeable armor. She admired these trees, she said, because they live in a land of little water and bitter cold, and they thrive on it—not unlike some of the characters in her stories. Both the men and the women in these stories are stubborn, crafty, and courageous. They are tenacious, and they do seem to thrive under adverse conditions. Sometimes they are delusional, but aren't we all, sometimes?

In the fall, winter, and spring, Carol lived reluctantly in New York City, mostly by herself, and wrote and taught. She kept in shape for summertime hiking by walking up the stairs to her apartment instead of taking the elevator. She lived on the twelfth floor. Among the many things I learned from Carol was that I too could walk to the twelfth floor.

Carol Emshwiller took me into the High Sierra in search of a pie shop and, in a separate adventure, made me an object of interest to the Inyo County Sheriff's Office. We found the pies, and we didn't get arrested. I can't say that she will subvert you in exactly the same way that she has me and William Gibson, but she will take you somewhere that expands your expectations, confronts your fears, and amuses you no end.

Terrible Trudy on the Lam

IT WAS A WHIM, a momentary desire to see what lay outside the zoo. But once Trudy had taken a walk around San Diego, once she'd tasted freedom, she was determined not to go back. She would make this work. At first, she lived in the city's lovely dark storm drains, emerging every night to forage for yummies in Balboa Park. But she knew her sylvan idyll would not last forever. She needed a long-term plan, and after a week of pondering the matter, she put one together.

A job was the first order of business, something that would keep her in shoots and leaves, and hopefully something she could do evenings: she was, of course, as the zookeepers had told her time and again, an odd-toed crepuscular ungulate. Twilight was her very best time of day, though she could go all night if she had to.

She considered roller skating. Bears do it, elephants do it, even penguins roller skate, and at that time roller-skating couples in evening dress were becoming a popular nightclub entertainment. Why not tapirs?

At first, Trudy thought maybe a prey-predator act would be exciting, since tapirs have been known to bite viciously when cornered, and that could be milked for comic effect. But tigers, the Malayan tapir's principle predator, rarely roller skate well. They consider it undignified, and often, when strapped into skates, just lie on their backs with their feet in the air, as if expecting a belly rub. Trudy considered putting together an act with another prey animal, but she was wary of partners: not every roller skater who said she was a vegetarian was committed to nonviolence. In the end, Trudy decided to go it alone.

A kindly shoemaker created custom open-toed roller skates for her, to show off her tiny hooved toes, three on each back foot, four on each foot in the front. The boots were made of red leather, which contrasted elegantly with Trudy's silver shoulders and black flanks. A black bowtie and a starched white collar pulled the whole ensemble together in a dignified and professional way. A refined Marlene Dietrich look, Trudy thought, right to the silver tracings on the tips of her ears.

She practiced skating late at night, after the rink had closed and everyone had gone home. It was dark, but tapirs have poor eyesight, and she was accustomed to tiptoeing around in a dusky forest. Eventually the groundskeeper discovered that she had broken into the rink through an unused storage closet, and the jig was up, but by then she had perfected a hilarious pantomime routine. She skittered out onto the dance floor, flailing about and threatening to crash into tables along its edge, then regaining her composure and performing a series of graceful loops and twirls, ending in an Axel, loop, double Mapes, Euler, double flip.

Audiences loved it—in performance, the finale always drew gasps from the tables—and they took Trudy to their hearts. San Diegans, grieving and distressed after the attack on Pearl Harbor the previous year, sought consolation in bars and supper clubs, and Terrible Trudy the Roller Skating Tapir was a hit. Hollywood celebrities flocked to San Diego, ostensibly to perform for the troops at the naval base, but really to catch Trudy's act at the Chi-Chi Supper Club, a hot new nightclub with a South Seas theme. Trudy sometimes added a lei to her costume; it also served as a midnight snack.

As Trudy's star rose, so did her worries about the zoo director, the indomitable Belle Benchley. Mrs. Benchley had pioneered the modern, natural-looking, cageless zoo. Trudy had rejected Benchley's carefully simulated enclosure, and Trudy's wanderlust had challenged the woman to the core. Mrs. Benchley knew Trudy was living in La Jolla and working openly at the Chi-Chi Club but had made no effort to contact her. How long would this détente last?

#

At first, Trudy seemed to be nonchalance itself. She flirted with members of the audience, of any gender, who caught her eye. If an object or an article of clothing attracted her interest, she would take possession of it, though she usually returned it to the owner at the end of her set. In such a fashion, she acquired a fedora, and she instantly made it a permanent part of her act. A huge fan of the singer Jimmy Durante, Trudy interspersed her spectacular skating-routine with Durante imitations, just as Durante would pause in the middle of a song and break into a quick comedy routine, then return to the song as if nothing had happened. Turns out she was a very affecting singer, with a sense of comedic timing that rivaled Durante's own. Not to mention she had a schnozzola that even Durante envied.

The crowds went wild.

But the stress began to tell on Trudy, who knew that at any moment Mrs. Benchley could, on a whim, decide to bring Trudy back to the zoo and its fake Malayan rainforest. Trudy had no legal leg to stand on: as she had been reminded by her lawyers time and again, she was the property of the San Diego Zoo. Trudy began downing a quick Tonga Punch—or maybe two—before the show, just to keep her courage up. One evening, she went a bit further than two, and had not sobered up by show time. She went on anyway rather than disappoint the crowd, and the revelers took her markedly sloppy routine as a clever commentary on the club MC, who was notorious for never showing up to work sober. People laughed and laughed, and their wild reception of her wacky skate-dance encouraged her to act out even more.

She was careening between the supper tables on one foot, waving the other three in the air, picking up customers' champagne glasses with her schnoz, and singing "Inka-dinka-do," when suddenly her luck ran out, and her wheels caught on a crack in the floor. Had she been sober and standing on all four feet, she could have recovered, but that was not the case.

Trudy went flying and landed on top of a table occupied by William Randolph Hearst and his paramour Marion Davies. Drenched in expensive champagne, Miss Davies fled the nightclub, leaving behind her ermine evening wrap and Mr. Hearst. As the newspapers told the story, Mr. Hearst immediately bestowed the ermine on Trudy, to console her for her embarrassment. Miss Davies later vowed publicly never again to leave either her clothing or her man alone in Trudy's presence, declaring, "That little rhinoceros minx has an elevated opinion of her own attractiveness." (Here we must acknowledge that, although tapirs and rhinoceroses are among the few odd-toed ungulates, tapirs are not rhinoceroses, and neither of them are minks.)

Trudy, realizing that her career as a headliner at the Chi-Chi had come to an end, saluted the audience with her fedora, adlibbed Durante's signature closing, "Good night, Mrs. Calabash, wherever you are," and lit out for LA as fast as she could travel, just one step ahead of Mrs. Benchley. She was only a tapir, making her lonely way in this dreadful world, but she knew when to call it a night.

#

It took just a couple hours to bus from San Diego to Los Angeles, and by midnight, Trudy, clutching her ermine stole about her, emerged from the Greyhound station on Los Angeles Street. She knew that pretty soon she'd need some kind of fake ID, but right then she sure hoped the cops wouldn't stop an innocent-looking young tapir in a classy fur wrap.

The few passengers on the late-night bus from San Diego scattered like roaches when you turn on the light. It was a quiet night, just a few people napped on the station's benches. No street traffic at all, really. Trudy was alone in LA, and had no real idea of where to go. She was pretty sure that LA had storm drains and that the gardens of Beverly Hills would provide sustenance. She was also under the impression that Beverly Hills was somewhere north of the Greyhound station, which was true enough. She struck out at once, heading north toward Olvera Street and what, she had heard, were some of the most colorful sections of the city. The wind was off the ocean, and she could smell the salt air.

After just a few blocks, she left the dreary bus-station-shabby street and entered a neighborhood of trim little wooden bungalows. It smelled good—it smelled edible in fact. Maybe she should have a nosh here, she thought. Why hold out for Beverly Hills? She reached for some greenery and was nibbling it delicately when she noticed a man in the shadows, crouched next to a 1937 Oldsmobile. The streetlights were dim and one to a block, but Trudy's eyesight was best in low-light situations, so she had no problem picking him out.

#

He was wearing a crumpled serge suit with an ugly striped tie that had slipped askew. His fedora was battered in a way that suggested he habitually sat on it. A pint of something alcoholic stuck out of his jacket pocket. He looked slightly dangerous and unmistakably up to no good. Trudy caught his eye.

He raised his eyebrows, nodded to Trudy, and, cool as a frozen daiquiri, brought his left index finger to his lips and gave her a stern cautionary glance. She nodded slightly in return. She would give him a chance to explain himself, she thought.

Then, suddenly, he leaped up, holding a huge flash camera in both hands, and aimed it into the back seat of the Olds, photographing the car's interior. The flash lit up the scene, and a high-pitched scream came from the car. The photographer broke away, ran like hell down the driveway right next to Trudy, and disappeared into a large privet hedge that Trudy had been considering for dessert.

The driver-side door of the Olds pushed open and a partly dressed guy jumped out, clutching a wrench. He spotted Trudy and shouted, "Where'd he go?" Trudy didn't care to be addressed so rudely. She gestured toward Beverly Hills, and he started down the street a few yards, then stopped. He turned around and came back to the car, buttoning his yellow-and-pink Hawaiian shirt, with a truculent look on his face.

"Get your things on, babe," he said to the person inside. "I'll take you home, and then I'll deal with the gumshoe." A woman said something low and mewly, but Trudy couldn't make out what it was. "I'll pay him off, that's what. I'll take care of him. Don't worry about it." He leaped into the car, started it, threw it in gear, and they clattered off down the street.

Trudy made her move on the privet, which was as tasty as she thought it would be.

The blackmailer, for that's surely what he was, emerged from the hedge. "They gone?" He kept his voice low, and he mumbled.

Trudy, her mouth full of fresh privet, simply nodded.

"I like a dame can keep her mouth shut," the man said. He held out his hand. "Name's Mumble," he said. "Firrup Mumble."

Trudy nodded again. That couldn't be his name, she knew, but it was really hard to understand him. No matter. She ignored his hand and continued to chew the privet.

"Divorce case," he said, tilting his head toward where the Olds had been parked. He lowered his hand. "That mug's been out with a different floozie every night. His ole lady'll take him for every penny he's got."

Trudy just looked at him. Not a blackmailer, a PI.

"You keep your own counsel, I can tell," said the man.

Trudy continued to keep her own counsel.

"You need a job, kid? You look hard up, wandering around in the middle of the night, eating people's shrubbery."

It was clear to Trudy that either he hadn't noticed the ermine stole or he thought it was part of a tapir's standard equipment, but the question, and the man's concern, softened her reserve. She nodded her head vigorously.

"I could use an assistant, someone who keeps their mouth shut, y' know'd I mean?"

Trudy shrugged, but didn't deny that she could keep her mouth shut.

"I'm a private dick, and I do mean private." He spoke a little louder, a little more clearly. "But I could use a dame to handle surveillance. You over eighteen?" Trudy nodded again, though actually she was only five. Seemed about right, though—just past adolescence.

"Well, come along then. Jalopy's over here. I gotta get these pix developed. Lady's gonna be filing for divorce, needs her flagrante delicto."

I don't want to be anybody's assistant, thought Trudy. I want to be the detective. I want to find the flagrante delictos. But I guess I'll deal with that later. She followed Firrup Mumble to his car.

#

And that was how Trudy happened to be in the front room of the detective's office later that night, filling out an application for a PI license, when the irate adulterer came by with a shotgun. She saw his blurred form through the pebbled-glass panel in the office door, and she recognized his pink-and-yellow shirt as the one on the guy who had driven off in the Olds just a few hours before.

Trudy was pretty sure that, whatever her job turned out to be, some of it would involve running interference when people with whom the private eye had dealt in a professional capacity dropped by to discuss matters. So she put down her pencil and waited for the knock.

The knock, it turned out, was the crash of the butt end of a shotgun coming through the pebbled glass. Trudy dashed forward, heedless of flying glass shards. The visitor aimed the shotgun directly into the PI's private office.

Trudy reached over with her prehensile proboscis and pushed down hard on the barrel. The gun went off and sent a load of buckshot through the open office door and right into the front of the detective's desk.

Trudy pressed her attack, making low-pitched, hollow grunts and emphasizing them with piercing whistles. She tilted her head back and waggled her long, phallic snout, raising it like an elephant's trunk to reveal, deep behind her huge fleshy lips, a set of choppers as blunt and massive as those of a horse. She gave the man an emphatic bite on the arm, then reached over with her snout and grabbed the shotgun right out of his hands.

The guy let it go. He seemed to have lost interest in it completely and was staring at Trudy in complete disbelief. The detective appeared at the door to his office, and his would-be assailant turned to him with a look of helpless appeal. "If that's a dog, it's the weirdest damn dog I've ever seen. What the hell *is* it?"

"My little sister. You got a problem?" The detective took the gun from Trudy and stashed it behind his desk.

"Your sister? It's got horse feet for toes! And it's wearing fur spats. It looks like two different animals put together, a white one in the front and a black one in the back." He seemed on the verge of hysteria.

"Y'know, buster, you look like you were put together from spare parts yourself. I don't think you oughta be insulting my sister's protective coloration. May I inquire as to the purpose of your visit?"

Trudy was surprised and pleased to hear the gumshoe defend her like that. She had thought he wasn't any too thrilled to be told that she wanted to be a detective. In her experience, men did not take kindly to females of any persuasion who aspired to their jobs. Perhaps this one was different.

"Gimme the negs," said the miscreant. "You know what's good for you, gimme them right now."

"You're not in a great position to make demands, buddy," said the detective. "You want, the cops can make you a set of prints suitable for framing."

The man leaped for the shotgun, but the quick-witted gumshoe kicked it away. Then the fellow pulled a knife.

Unarmed and taken by surprise, the detective grabbed an office chair and raised it, to keep his attacker at a distance, but it was clear to Trudy that he was not going to win a fight against a thug with a knife.

She looked about for a weapon, or at least something she could grab and throw. Her eye fell upon her ermine stole. It was fluffy and soft and white, a garment that made her feel like the cutest little bunny in the world, but she knew that ermines were basically weasels in white coats. Vicious. The stole would distract the knife-wielding adulterer, perhaps tapping into an atavistic human fear of the weasel.

Trudy grabbed the stole with her snout and waved it, as if teasing a bull, to get the intruder's attention. He looked up and stared at her in baffled panic: what was the beast doing now? Trudy flung the stole at the intruder, and it wrapped fuzzily around his head, like a flying squirrel. The detective quickly picked up the shotgun and hit the knife out of the panicked miscreant's hand.

Five minutes later, the fellow was neatly trussed and tied to the chair, and Trudy, wrapped again in the ermine, sat with her new boss on the wooden anteroom bench, awaiting the arrival of Detective Lieutenant Breeze.

The detective poured them each a shot of Old Forrester.

"You got it, kid," he said, tipping his glass toward her. "You're coolheaded, aware of your surroundings, and deft at improvised distraction. I'll see that your PI certification is approved." He downed his glass, then poured another one. "You've got a job here with me as long as you want it, if you don't mind occasional gunplay."

Trudy thought about it. She knew there would come a day when she would flee the dark, cynical world of the LA gumshoe, just as she'd fled the sleepy San Diego Zoo and the tacky ritz of the Chi-Chi Club. It might well involve gunplay and hot pursuit, and that was okay with her.

The thing you want when you're a prey animal, Trudy thought, is intermittent excitement. She could have a decent, happy life as the occasional target of someone's violent intentions, because she loved the pure energy of being chased. She bore no malice toward those pursuing her, and her heart soared at every triumphant escape. She wondered if Mumble, whatever his name was, who like most detectives lived for the chase, would understand. Maybe she'd ask him sometime, but not now.

Trudy nodded to Firrup Mumble and took a sip of bourbon. She smiled a hidden tapir smile. Mrs. Benchley might yet track her down, but for the time being she had escaped. And she had a job. Life was good.

Author's note

Terrible Trudy was a resident of the San Diego Zoo in the 1940s and '50s. Her escapes caught the popular imagination, but eventually zoo director Belle Benchley tracked her down and persuaded her to return and stay put. Trudy died of comfortable old age in 1959, in retirement at a rainforest habitat in the San Diego Zoo. Mrs. Benchley, influential in her advocacy of humane animal habitats for zoos, followed in 1972.

Bibliography

Books

Night Shift. Oakland: PM Press, 2022.

Questionable Practices. Easthampton, MA: Small Beer Press, 2014.

Stable Strategies and Others. San Francisco: Tachyon, 2004.

Anthologies

The WisCon Chronicles, Vol. 2: Provocative Essays on Feminism, Race, Revolution, and the Future. Edited with L. Timmel Duchamp. Seattle: Aqueduct Press, 2008.

Online Magazines

Flurb: A Webzine of Astonishing Tales no. 11, Spring–Summer, 2011. Guest editor, single issue. *Flurb* was an online fiction magazine founded and edited by Rudy Rucker. An archive of each issue is available at https://flurb.net.

The Infinite Matrix

Editor and publisher, August 2000–July 2008. *The Infinite Matrix* was an online fiction and news magazine, updated daily and archived monthly. An archive of stories and articles is available at http://infinitematrix.net.

GORP

Managing editor, September 1998–January 2000. GORP (The Great Outdoor Recreation Pages) was a mammoth resource on outdoor activities around the world. It published forty stories a month. There is no archive.

Fiction

"Terrible Trudy on the Lam." *Asimov's Science Fiction*, March–April 2019.

"Night Shift." *Visions, Ventures, Velocities: A Collection of Space Futures*, edited by Joey Eschrich, Ed Finn, and Juliet Ulman. Tempe, AZ: Center for Science and the Imagination, 2017.

"Application for Asylum." *Welcome to Dystopia*, edited by Gordon Van Gelder. New York: OR Books, 2017.

"Transitions." *Seat 14C* webzine, edited by Kathryn Cramer. X-Prize, October 2017.

"Face Value." *Readercon 24 Souvenir Book*, edited by Richard Duffy and Ellen Brody. Readercon, 2013.

"Hive Mind Man," with Rudy Rucker. *Asimov's Science Fiction*, February 2012.

"The Collector of Neckties." *New York Review of Science Fiction*, December 2011.

"After the Thaw." *Flurb: A Webzine of Astonishing Tales* no. 12, Fall–Winter 2011.

"Thought Experiment." *Eclipse Four: New Science Fiction and Fantasy*, edited by Jonathan Strahan. San Francisco: Night Shade Books, 2011.

"The Trains That Climb the Winter Tree," with Michael Swanwick. *Tor. com*, December 21, 2010.

"Internal Devices." *Tor.com*, November 2, 2010.

"The Perdido Street Project." *Tor.com*, November 1, 2010.

"Day after the Cooters." *Tor.com*, October 29, 2010.

"A Different Engine." *Tor.com*, October 28, 2010.

"Zeppelin City," with Michael Swanwick. *Tor.com*, November 6, 2009.

"The Armies of Elfland," with Michael Swanwick. *Asimov's Science Fiction*, April–May 2009.

"Shed That Guilt! Double Your Productivity Overnight!," with Michael Swanwick. *The Magazine of Fantasy and Science Fiction*, 2008.

"Up the Fire Road." *Eclipse One*, edited by Jonathan Strahan. San Francisco: Night Shade Books, 2007.

"No Place to Raise Kids: A Tale of Forbidden Love." *Flurb: A Webzine of Astonishing Tales* no. 3, Spring–Summer, 2007.

"Michael Swanwick and Samuel R. Delany at the Joyce Kilmer Service Area, March 2005." *Foundation* no. 101, 2007.

"Speak, Geek." *Nature*, August 24, 2006.

"Nirvana High," with Leslie What. *Asimov's Science Fiction*, September 2004.

"Coming to Terms." *Asimov's Science Fiction*, September 2004.

"Green Fire," with Andy Duncan, Pat Murphy, and Michael Swanwick. *Event Horizon Online*, January 1999.

"Fellow Americans." *Asimov's Science Fiction*, December 1991.

"Lichen and Rock." *Asimov's Science Fiction*, June 1991.

"The Sock Story." *Asimov's Science Fiction*, September 1989.

"Computer Friendly." *Asimov's Science Fiction*, June 1989.

"Stable Strategies for Middle Management." *Asimov's Science Fiction*, June 1988.

"Spring Conditions." *Tales by Moonlight*, edited by Jessica Amanda Salmonson. Chicago: Robert T. Garcia, 1983.

"Contact." *Proteus: Voices for the 80s*, edited by Richard S. McEnroe. New York: Ace SF, 1981.

"What Are Friends For?" *Amazing Stories*, November 1978.

"Deaf Ted, Danoota & Me (& Our Friend Malcolm & Our Faithful Frog Besideus) Fight the Grorks." *Ethos* 41, no. 2, May 1967. Emmanuel College.

"George the Orange Tree." *Ethos*, 1966. Emmanuel College.

"The Cage." *Ethos* 41, no. 1, December 1966. Emmanuel College.

Poems

"To the Moon Alice." *Lady Churchill's Rosebud Wristlet*, June 2008.

Nonfiction

Introduction to *Neuromancer* by William Gibson. Lakewood, CO: Centipede Press, 2022.

"Going Through an Impasse: Evading Writer's Block." *Pocket Workshop: Essays on Living as a Writer*, edited by Tod McCoy and M. Huw Evans. Seattle: Hydra House, 2021.

"The Pleasures of Reading, Viewing, and Listening in 2021: Eileen Gunn." *Ambling Along the Aqueduct*, Aqueduct Press, https://ambling37.rssing.com/. See also "The Pleasures of . . ." posts by Gunn for *Ambling Along the Aqueduct* for the years 2007, 2008, 2010, 2013, 2019, and 2020.

"Robots and Cheerios." Introduction to electronic edition of *The Tomorrow Makers* by Grant Fermedal, 2020.

"Memories of Gardner." Gardner Dozois, *On the Road with Gardner Dozois: Travel Narratives 1995–2000*. Edited by Erin Underwood and Tony Lewis. Framingham, MA: NESFA Press, 2019.

"A Remembrance of Vonda M. McIntyre." *Remembering Vonda*, edited by Stephanie A. Smith and Jeanne Gomoll. Madison, WI: Union Street Press, 2019.

"So How Do You Know Rudy?" Introduction to *Turing and Burroughs* by Rudy Rucker. New York: Night Shade Books, 2019.

"Quiet Gardner Dozois." *New York Review of Science Fiction* no. 349, November 2018.

"Memories of Kate Wilhelm." *Locus Magazine* no. 687, April 2018.

"Celebrating 50 Years of Locus." *Locus Magazine* no. 687, April 2018.

Annotations for *Frankenstein: Annotated for Scientists, Engineers, and Creators of All Kinds*, edited by David H. Guston, Ed Finn, and Jason Scott Robert. Cambridge, MA: MIT Press, 2017.

"Thirteen Ways of Looking at Pat Cadigan." *MidAmeriCon II Souvenir Book*, 2016. https://fanac.org/conpubs/Worldcon/MidAmeriCon%202/Mac2%20Program%20Book.pdf.

"Diversity and the Infinite Matrix." *The WisCon Chronicles, Vol. 9: Intersections and Alliances*, edited by Mary Anne Mohanraj. Seattle: Aqueduct Press, 2015.

"American Authors in China," with Ellen Datlow and Michael Swanwick. *Locus Magazine* no. 653, June 2015.

"How America's Leading Science Fiction Authors Are Shaping Your Future." *Smithsonian*, May 2014.

"Five SF Stories about Linotype Machines." *Locus Magazine*, October 24, 2013.

"Dallying with Datlow," with Nancy Kress. *LoneStarCon3: The 71st World Science Fiction Convention*, 2013.

"'Hey, It's Bob': A Remembrance of Robert Morales." *Locus Magazine* no. 629, June 2013.

Preface to *The Wailing of the Gaulish Dead*. Upper Montclair, NJ: Nutmeg Point District Mail, 2013.

"Paul Williams." *Locus Magazine* no. 628, May 2013.

"In Memory of Joanna Russ: Tributes from WisCon 35," with L. Timmel Duchamp, Jeanne Gomoll, Farah Mendlesohn, Geoff Ryman, and Amy Thomson, *The WisCon Chronicles, Vol. 6: Futures of Feminism and Fandom*, edited by Alexis Lothian. Seattle: Aqueduct Press, 2012.

"The Irresistibly Readable Katherine MacLean." *Readercon Souvenir Book*, Readercon, July 2012.

"Stable Strategies for Middle Management." *Kafkaesque: Stories Inspired by Franz Kafka*, edited by John Kessel and James Patrick Kelly. San Francisco: Tachyon, 2011.

"On Joanna Russ and WisCon." *Chunga* no. 18, December 2011.

"Visions of Joanna: Remembering Joanna Russ." *Locus Magazine*, June 2011.

"Going to Narrative." Introduction to *Narrative Power: Encounters, Celebrations, Struggles*, edited by L. Timmel Duchamp. Seattle: Aqueduct Press, 2010.

"'The Author' and the author and the aspirant." *80! Memories and Reflections on Usual K. Le Guin*, edited by Karen Joy Fowler and Debbie Notkin. Seattle: Aqueduct Press, 2010.

"As the Twig Is Bent." *New York Review of Science Fiction*, May 2010.

"Michael Swanwick: The Last Modest Man." *World Fantasy Convention, 2009* souvenir book, edited by Eleanor Farrell, Patrick Swenson, and Rina Weisman, World Fantasy Convention, 2009.

"Where Everything Is a Bit Different." Introduction to *Filter House* by Nisi Shawl, Aqueduct Press, 2008.

"Japan Welcomes the World." *Locus Magazine* no. 562, November 2007.

"Eurocon 2006: Books and Food in a City of Passionate Readers." *Locus Magazine* no. 547, August, 2006.

"Cranking the Wheel of Reality." Introduction to *Last Week's Apocalypse*, by Douglas Lain, Nightshade Books, 2006.

"Letter from Eileen Gunn to Oscar Wilde." *Talking Back: Epistolary Fantasies*, Aqueduct Press, 2006.

"A Tour of Chernobyl, April 2006." *The Infinite Matrix*, April 26, 2006.

"Kiss kiss! Bang bang!" *The Infinite Matrix*, January 23, 2006.

"Approaching Oblivion." *The Infinite Matrix*, December 30, 2005.

"Do Not Remove This Tag." Introduction to *I Live With You*, by Carol Emshwiller, Tachyon Publications, 2005.

"Alone in the Kitchen: Computers, Freedom, and Privacy." *The Infinite Matrix*, April 15, 2005.

"On 'Coming to Terms.'" *SFWA Bulletin* 38, no. 4, 2005, edited by Mark Kreighbaum.

"Science Fiction Museum and Hall of Fame." *Locus Magazine* no. 523, August 2004.

"Curious Damon Knight." *Nebula Awards Showcase 2004*, Roc/New American Library, 2004.

"Survivor! Two Years of the Infinite Matrix." *The Infinite Matrix*, August 1, 2003.

"Science Fiction Vital to Homeland Security." *The Infinite Matrix*, April 2, 2003.

"A Year of Living Dangerously." *The Infinite Matrix*, November 20, 2002.

"Back from the Dead!" *The Infinite Matrix*, November 19, 2001.

"Hail and Farewell." *The Infinite Matrix*, August 1, 2001.

"What I Know About Michael Swanwick." *Readercon 13 Souvenir Book*, edited by Bob Colby, Bob Ingria, Sheila Lightsey, Michael Matthew, and Eric Van. Readercon, July 2001.

"Alternate Waldrops." *Strange Horizons*, January 29, 2001.

"Avram Davidson: Water from a Deep Well." *Everybody Has Somebody in Heaven: Essential Jewish Tales of the Spirit*, edited by Grania David and Jack Dann. New York: Devora Publishing, 2000.

Introduction to "The Affair at Lahore Cantonment." *The Avram Davidson Treasury: A Tribute Collection*, edited by Robert Silverberg and Grania Davidson. New York: Tor, 1998.

"Vonda N. McIntyre: The Real Story." *Lunacon Program Book*, Lunacon, 1994.

"The Hacker Crackdown: Law and Disorder on the Electronic Frontier." *Science Fiction Eye* no. 11, December 1992.

"There's No Place Like Home," with Kathleen Ann Goonan. *The New York Review of Science Fiction*, November 1992.

"Ideologically Labile Fruit Crisp." *The Bakery Men Don't See*, edited by Jeanne Gomoll and Diane Martin, SF3, 1991.

"A Difference Dictionary." *Science Fiction Eye* no. 8, Winter 1991.

Interviews by Eileen Gunn

"Interview with Nisi Shawl." In *Something More and More* by Nisi Shawl. Seattle: Aqueduct Press, 2011.

"SF in Mexico: A Chat with Bef," with Bernardo Fernández. *Locus Magazine* no. 588, January 2010.

"Interview of Geoff [Ryman]." In *What Remains* by Ellen Klages and Geoff Ryman. Seattle: Aqueduct Press, 2009.

"The WisCon Questions: A Coven of People Who Attended WisCon 30 Answer Random Personal Questions Posed by Eileen Gunn," with Tempest Bradford, Suzy Charnas, Ted Chiang, Carol Emshwiller, Jeanne Gomoll, Liz Henry, Ellen Klages, Ursula K. Le Guin, Spike Parsons, Julie Phillips, Mark Rich, Diantha Day Sprouse, and Lisa Tuttle. In *The WisCon Chronicles, Vol. 1*, edited by. L. Timmel Duchamp. Seattle: Aqueduct Press, 2007.

About the Author

Eileen Gunn is a science-fiction writer and editor based in Seattle, Washington. Her work has received the Nebula Award in the United States and the Sense of Gender award in Japan, and has been nominated for the Hugo, Nebula, World Fantasy, Philip K. Dick, Tiptree, and Locus awards in the United States.

From 2001 to 2008, she was editor and publisher of the *Infinite Matrix* webzine, one of the earliest science-fiction webzines, which published stories by both major writers and newcomers. She had previously served as managing editor for GORP.com, a huge website that provided in-depth information about global resources for outdoor recreation and published forty stories a month covering sports and destinations all over the world.

In her earlier career, in technology advertising, Gunn wrote ads for the first minicomputers in the late 1960s. Later, in the mid-1980s, she served as director of advertising and sales promotion at Microsoft. Her advertising career spanned thirty-four years of rapid change in computer and communications technology.

Gunn also teaches occasional writing workshops, focusing on managing the creative process and its interruptions. She attended the Clarion Writers Workshop in 1976 and attended the casual monthly pro workshops run by Kate Wilhelm and Damon Knight in Eugene, Oregon. She served twenty-two years on the board of directors of the Clarion West Writers Workshop and taught a week each at the summer workshops in 2015 and 2021. She now serves on the board of directors of the Locus Foundation.

FRIENDS OF

These are indisputably momentous times—the financial system is melting down globally and the Empire is stumbling. Now more than ever there is a vital need for radical ideas.

In the years since its founding—and on a mere shoestring—PM Press has risen to the formidable challenge of publishing and distributing knowledge and entertainment for the struggles ahead. With hundreds of releases to date, we have published an impressive and stimulating array of literature, art, music, politics, and culture. Using every available medium, we've succeeded in connecting those hungry for ideas and information to those putting them into practice.

Friends of PM allows you to directly help impact, amplify, and revitalize the discourse and actions of radical writers, filmmakers, and artists. It provides us with a stable foundation from which we can build upon our early successes and provides a much-needed subsidy for the materials that can't necessarily pay their own way. You can help make that happen—and receive every new title automatically delivered to your door once a month—by joining as a Friend of PM Press. And, we'll throw in a free T-shirt when you sign up.

Here are your options:

- $30 a month: Get all books and pamphlets plus 50% discount on all webstore purchases
- $40 a month: Get all PM Press releases (including CDs and DVDs) plus 50% discount on all webstore purchases
- $100 a month: Superstar—Everything plus PM merchandise, free downloads, and 50% discount on all webstore purchases

For those who can't afford $30 or more a month, we have Sustainer Rates at $15, $10, and $5. Sustainers get a free PM Press T-shirt and a 50% discount on all purchases from our website.

Your Visa or Mastercard will be billed once a month, until you tell us to stop. Or until our efforts succeed in bringing the revolution around. Or the financial meltdown of Capital makes plastic redundant. Whichever comes first.

PM Press is an independent, radical publisher of books and media to educate, entertain, and inspire. Founded in 2007 by a small group of people with decades of publishing, media, and organizing experience, PM Press amplifies the voices of radical authors, artists, and activists. Our aim is to deliver bold political ideas and vital stories to all walks of life and arm the dreamers to demand the impossible. We have sold millions of copies of our books, most often one at a time, face to face. We're old enough to know what we're doing and young enough to know what's at stake. Join us to create a better world.

PM Press
PO Box 23912
Oakland, CA 94623
info@pmpress.org

PM Press in Europe
europe@pmpress.org
www.pmpress.org.uk

PM PRESS OUTSPOKEN AUTHORS

JOHN CROWLEY
TOTALITOPIA
Plus...

"I wish I had his imagination for ten ordinary writers."

PM PRESS OUTSPOKEN AUTHORS

SAMUEL R. DELANY
THE ATHEIST IN
THE ATTIC
Plus...

"A talent very close to time travel—or magic."
—LOCUS

PM PRESS OUTSPOKEN AUTHORS

MICHAEL BLUMLEIN
THOREAU'S MICROSCOPE
Plus...

"Blumlein has an exceptional vision, and he
conveys it with exceptional talent."
—WASHINGTON POST

PM PRESS OUTSPOKEN AUTHORS

RACHEL POLLACK
THE BEATRIX GATES
Plus...

"Here is magic... A big strange create concentrated."
—SAMUEL DELANY, AUTHOR OF NOVA

PM PRESS OUTSPOKEN AUTHORS

PAUL PARK
A CITY MADE OF WORDS
Plus...

"A brilliant, stunning, frightening display of talent."
—GENE WOLFE

PM PRESS OUTSPOKEN AUTHORS

NISI SHAWL
TALK LIKE A MAN
Plus...

"Shawl is brilliant."
—AMAL EL-MOHTAR, NPR.ORG

PM PRESS OUTSPOKEN AUTHORS

MEG ELISON
BIG GIRL
Plus...

"Compelling and fierce and unstoppable."
—PAT MURPHY, WORLD FANTASY AWARD WINNER

PM PRESS OUTSPOKEN AUTHORS

NICK MAMATAS
THE PLANETBREAKER'S SON
Plus...

"One of the most innovative, fascinating,
and distinctive voices in the field."
—LOCUS MAGAZINE

PM PRESS OUTSPOKEN AUTHORS

VANDANA SINGH
UTOPIAS OF THE THIRD KIND

"One of the most compelling and forceful voices in recent SF."
—GARY K. WOLFE, LOCUS